**Amalie Skram** (1846-1905) is one of Norway's major nineteenth-century novelists. Her turbulent early life in the bustling seaport of Bergen, and then travelling the world as the wife of a ship's captain, gave her ample material for her studies of modern life, and in particular her portrayals of women's struggles against restricted freedom and stifling convention. Novels like *Constance Ring* (1885), *Lucie* (1888) and *Betrayed* (1892) focus on the double standard of sexual morality and its consequences for the young women – and men – whose lives are blighted by it. The four-novel cycle *The People of Hellemyr* (1887-98) is a Zolaesque portrayal of the doomed attempt of a family to escape the vicious circle of poverty and crime. *Fru Inés* (1891) is unusual amongst her novels in being set in Constantinople; the chaotic life of this cosmopolitan melting-pot forms a rich background to a tale of passion and despair.

**Katherine Hanson** and **Judith Messick** have been translating together since the 1980s. They began with Amalie Skram's *Constance Ring*, followed by her asylum novels, *Professor Hieronimus* and *St. Jørgen's* (English title: *Under Observation*), and the marriage novel *Lucie*. Hanson and Messick have also researched Skram's correspondence and written articles on her letters to publishers and friends.

Katherine Hanson received her Ph.D in Scandinavian Languages and Literature at the University of Washington. She has taught Norwegian language and Scandinavian literature at St. Olaf College Pacific Lutheran University and the University of Washington where she is currently an Affiliate Associate Professor.

Judith Messick has a Ph.D in English Literature from the University of California, where she taught for several years. In 1992 she joined the Kellogg School for Management at Northwestern University. She retired in 2001. Her interest in Amalie Skram dates back to the mid-1970s when she and her family lived in Bergen.

## Some other books from Norvik Press

Jens Bjørneboe: *Moment of Freedom* (translated by Esther Greenleaf Mürer)

Jens Bjørneboe: *Powderhouse* (translated by Esther Greenleaf Mürer)

Jens Bjørneboe: *The Silence* (translated by Esther Greenleaf Mürer)

Johan Borgen: *The Scapegoat* (translated by Elizabeth Rokkan)

Kerstin Ekman: *Witches' Rings* (translated by Linda Schenck)

Kerstin Ekman: *The Spring* (translated by Linda Schenck)

Kerstin Ekman: *The Angel House* (translated by Sarah Death)

Kerstin Ekman: *City of Light* (translated by Linda Schenck)

Arne Garborg: *The Making of Daniel Braut* (translated by Marie Wells)

Svava Jakobsdóttir: *Gunnlöth's Tale* (translated by Oliver Watts)

P. C. Jersild: *A Living Soul* (translated by Rika Lesser)

Selma Lagerlöf: *Lord Arne's Silver* (translated by Sarah Death)

Selma Lagerlöf: *The Löwensköld Ring* (translated by Linda Schenck)

Selma Lagerlöf: *The Phantom Carriage* (translated by Peter Graves)

Viivi Luik: *The Beauty of History* (translated by Hildi Hawkins)

Henry Parland: *To Pieces* (translated by Dinah Cannell)

Amalie Skram: *Lucie* (translated by Katherine Hanson and Judith Messick)

Amalie and Erik Skram: *Caught in the Enchanter's Net: Selected Letters* (edited and translated by Janet Garton)

August Strindberg: *Tschandala* (translated by Peter Graves)

August Strindberg: *The Red Room* (translated by Peter Graves)

Hjalmar Söderberg: *Martin Birck's Youth* (translated by Tom Ellett)

Hjalmar Söderberg: *Selected Stories* (translated by Carl Lofmark)

Anton Tammsaare: *The Misadventures of the New Satan* (translated by Olga Shartze and Christopher Moseley)

Elin Wägner: *Penwoman* (translated by Sarah Death)

# Fru Inés

by

Amalie Skram

Translated from the Norwegian
and with a Translators' Note by
Katherine Hanson and Judith Messick

Norvik Press
2014

Originally published as *Fru Inés* in 1891 by Schubothe Forlag, Copenhagen.

This translation and Translators' Afterword © Katherine Hanson and Judith Messick 2014.
The translators' moral right to be identified as the translators of the work has been asserted.

Norvik Press Series B: English Translations of Scandinavian Literature, no. 60

*A catalogue record for this book is available from the British Library.*

ISBN: 978-1-909408-05-0

Norvik Press gratefully acknowledges the generous support of NORLA and Institusjonen Fritt Ord towards the publication of this translation.

Norvik Press
Department of Scandinavian Studies
University College London
Gower Street
London WC1E 6BT
United Kingdom
Website: www.norvikpress.com
E-mail address: norvik.press@ucl.ac.uk

Managing editors: Sarah Death, Helena Forsås-Scott, Janet Garton, C. Claire Thomson.

Cover design: Elettra Carbone

Cover image: *Gatubild från Konstantinopel* (Street View from Constantinople), watercolour by Fritz von Dardel, 1886. Nordiska Museet, Stockholm. Photographer: Ann-Marie Eriksson

Layout: Marita Fraser

# Contents

## *Fru Inés*

*Plan of Constantinople* by C. Stolpe, 1882

# I

Breakfast was over at the Sultan Achmet Hotel on Prinkipo Island in the Sea of Marmara, and a majority of the spa guests had retired to comfortable chairs on the veranda, which surrounded on three sides a pale grey building with many brightly-colored awnings over the windows. Most of the guests were leaning back with cigarettes between their lips, drowsy in the heat, as they gazed out over the sparkling Sea of Marmara, where several hundred feet below, steamers glided past white sailing ships as if they were pulled by wires, and in the distance Constantinople's white minarets and glittering domes rose above the city's violet-gold mist.

In the center of the veranda, facing a wide, densely-shaded marble staircase that led down to the sea path from the hotel terrace high above, was a long marble table at which a woman with sparkling black eyes and coral jewelry was seated, dressed in a white morning gown of Persian silk, surrounded by as many men as could find a place at the table, while over in the corner where a couple of old myrtle trees drooped over the balustrade, a tall lean gentleman was lying back in a rocking chair, his face covered with a handkerchief and his thin narrow hands resting on his bony knees.

Talk was lively at the table across from the marble staircase. The woman led the conversation; every few seconds she took the cigarette out of her mouth and held it between her index and middle fingers, and every few seconds the gentlemen competed to light it. All sat leaning forward with their faces inclined toward her, as if they couldn't get enough of looking and listening, laughing and clapping their hands at whatever she said and conversing with her in different languages. The woman spoke fluent French, but veered often into Italian,

Spanish, English, and even Greek. Now and then she would suddenly address a few words of Swedish to a very young man with tightly curled hair, broad shoulders, and a narrow blond mustache. He was more reserved than the others, but his eyes were fixed on her face with a shy, fascinated expression. Occasionally he glanced up at an open window on the second floor, out of which two dark-haired girls were poking their heads, whispering and excitedly following what was happening at the lively woman's table.

'Perhaps you've heard this already?' the woman broke off the story she had begun, turning toward the young Swede, who blushed like a young girl.

'No, Fru Consulinde.'

'Just call me Fru Inés; that's what I prefer, and it's also customary in your country.'

'Ah, Fru Inés! Madame said "Fru Inés",' exclaimed one of the gentlemen in delight; he was wearing the suit of a Turkish civil servant. 'I know speak Swedish.'

'But really, don't you think the man must have been mad?' Inés said, picking up the broken thread of her story. 'Keeping one of his poor wives locked up because he caught her being too familiar with a eunuch, and a half-grown one at that. How could he be harmed by that?'

'*Brava Brava!*' Laughter rang out around her. Rapping the table enthusiastically with his open hand was a deeply tanned Spaniard dressed like a Turkish dandy, newly arrived from Paris, his bald head not quite hidden by his fez.

'Stop that,' Inés said, tapping his hand with her tortoise-shell cigarette case. 'We're not at a French cabaret, Señor.'

'Pardon me, beautiful Señorita,' he begged in a humble tone, and with a smile lifted his hand to his fez in a salute.

'And that poor fool of a eunuch,' Inés went on. 'Imagine being whipped in full view of the servants for an offense he has no concept of.'

'Ha, ha, ha!' they applauded.

'It's nothing to laugh at, gentlemen,' Inez said eagerly. 'Wouldn't it be outrageous to punish a lapdog — even if it was a male dog — because it follows orders and amuses its

*Monastery, Princes' Islands,* Steel engraving, 1838

mistress?'

'If only I were a lapdog,' a slender gentleman lamented in Italian. He had a birdlike face and limp moustaches that reached down to his lapels. His tawny deep-set eyes darted back and forth, and when no one laughed, he resumed his former infatuated gaze at Fru Inés.

'Become a Buddist,' Inés said mockingly, 'then you'll become an animal when you die. An ape I think,' she added in Swedish with a merry glance at Flemming.

'I'd gladly become a cannibal,' answered the Italian, clapping his hand against his hollow chest, 'if only Señorita Inés would keep me company.'

'I'm Roman Catholic, mind you, and a sincere believer,' Inés said, suddenly serious, looking as if in her thoughts she was making the sign of the cross. 'And really, I don't like this flippant tone. Remember we have an innocent young gentleman in our midst and we have to set him a good example.'

'Two, Mrs. Ribbing,' remarked a tall, well-built fellow with a wide beardless face, wearing English sporting clothes. He was sitting across from Flemming and had several times tried in vain to insert himself in the conversation by making jokes in English.

'I'm not worried about you,' Inés said brusquely. 'You're already quite corrupted I'm sure. But your friend — how old is Flemming, Mr. Konrad?'

'Twenty-two, he says, but he's lying of course — that's some ten years older than he really is, eh young Flemming?' Konrad aimed a paper pellet at Flemming's face, but Flemming brushed it aside with a forced little laugh.

'Just think, Mrs. Ribbing, he's never been in love. On my honor! At first I thought he was joking. Look how red he's getting.'

'You can be sure plenty have been in love with him,' Inés said dryly, rolling herself a new cigarette.

'For Heaven's sake, Mrs. Ribbing, spare him,' the Englishman begged anxiously. 'He suffers from attacks that come on when he gets emotionally upset. You really should ask the waiter to have an ice bag ready for his head. It flares up very fast.'

Inés said something in Greek to a fat little man across the table who was wearing elegant white clothes and a head covering of pale felt, like the flowerpot-shaped hats of the Dervishes.

'Ladies and gentlemen. The donkeys are here!' announced a Negro waiter from the hotel's open glass door, disappearing as soundlessly as he had come.

'Donkeys are here!' could be heard like a call to action all along the veranda, and everybody stood up except for the men at Inés's table and the tall lean man in the rocking chair.

'Are you listening, gentlemen? The donkeys are here.' Inés rapped on the table with her firm little hand, looking from one to the other. 'Go quickly or the others will get the best donkeys.'

'Oh, do come with us, Madame! How can you be so cruel?'

'Of course, Mrs. Ribbing is just joking. Why else would we have arranged this tour?'

Inés shook her head.

'Oh Señora, most beautiful of women, how can you have the heart to do this?' The Spaniard sprang up, went down on one knee and raised his hands imploringly toward Inés.

'Yes, let's kneel!' cried the Italian, casting himself down beside the Spaniard. 'Then our magnificent tyrant's heart will melt.'

'Stop this nonsense,' Inés waved her hand. 'Señor Antonio still thinks he's in a French cabaret.'

'Oh Señora, Señora, how cruelly you're treating me today,' complained the Spaniard, getting to his feet. 'Say you forgive me.'

'Yes, but then go, and take the others with you. — What are you doing down there?' She looked scornfully at the kneeling Italian. 'You've turned into a parrot, I do believe, and you're not even dead yet.'

'Madame, you wish to insult me,' the Italian said softly in rapid-fire French, getting to his feet and widening his beady eyes so that his large crooked nose took on a severe and threatening aspect.

Inés laughed, a deep and unrestrained laugh. 'Oh listen, gentlemen, may I count on you to be my seconds? Señor André and I shall have a duel!'

'Oh, she's divine!' André exclaimed with an unctuous smile and minced off waving his hand.

'Ladies and gentlemen, they're asking how many are in the party,' they heard in accented English from the Negro waiter at the door. 'They're saying too many donkeys have been ordered, and they're carrying on like the Dervishes over in Skutari.'

'All right, we'll be there in a moment,' Konrad nodded. 'Come along gentlemen! Mrs. Ribbing isn't going to California while we're gone.'

'Not even to Constantinople,' said Inés.

'Ah well, since we have no other choice.'

'*Au revoir*, Madame.'

'Good afternoon, Mrs. Ribbing.'

'*Addio*, Señorita.'

'*Addio*, Señora.'

'*Adieu*, Madame.'

'And what about you?' Inés put her arms on the table when the others had gone, leaned forward and looked at Flemming, who still remained seated.

He cast his eyes down and squirmed uncomfortably in his chair. 'So you're not coming along, Fru Inés,' he stammered.

'No, I don't feel like it. I made that tour once and that was more than enough. You come back completely done in, covered in sticky red dust, and in that heat! And you mustn't think there is anything to see. The monastery is a wretched little wooden hovel and the monks look like dirty baboons. Oh but the view, of course, you absolutely must go up there! All the foreigners make that tour.'

'Oh, I don't care about that,' Flemming mumbled.

'What's this? Surely you're not thinking about backing out? What would the two lovesick Fräuleins say — you're supposed to escort one of them, and you can rest assured, she won't let you get away.'

Flemming glanced surreptitiously up at the window on the

second floor. Inés turned her head and followed the direction of his gaze, then quickly turned back to Flemming and bit her little finger.

'There you see, now we have a scandal. Why didn't you give me a signal? You knew perfectly well that they were hanging halfway out of the window, listening and rolling their eyes.'

'Are you coming then, Herr Flemming?' a sarcastic German female voice called down from above. 'Or perhaps you'd rather not.'

'Of course! What makes you think he can manage to tear himself away, Berthe,' a second speaker immediately chimed in from the same place, then sang in a loud mocking voice,

'There is an island
Where the sirens dwell.'

And then complete silence.

'Have they gone?' Inés whispered.

'Yes,' Flemming answered after furtively glancing up.

'Well, I must say!' Inés leaned back in her chair and laughed the same unrestrained laugh as before. 'You know,' she continued, and her expression changed, 'they really were very rude, the cheeky little things.'

'Juveniles,' Flemming muttered, stroking his narrow mustache.

'Why don't you just go?!' Inés cried, gesturing as if she would push him away with both hands.

'What the devil's become of you, Arthur! Your lady is waiting for you!' It was Konrad calling from inside the hotel.

Flemming still didn't move.

'All right, I'm going now, so you can stay here by yourself.' Inés put her cigarette case in her pocket.

Flemming stood up, removed his hat and bowed. Then he walked slowly across the veranda.

Suddenly Inés pushed back her chair and sprang after him. 'Fool them and stay here,' she said with an eager, laughing face, and grabbed his arm. 'That would annoy the juveniles no end. Do you want to?'

'Yes.' He gazed at her with radiant eyes.

'This way,' she ran back across the veranda, followed by Flemming. 'Oh, this will be fun! You've disappeared, completely disappeared, and I have no idea where you are.' They slipped around the corner of the hotel and came to a little projecting *karnap* supported by white columns with walls of colored glass.

'In there, and hide behind the plants in the corner.' She opened the door with her knee and pushed him through the opening. 'Nobody will come here because it connects to our sitting room. Shhh, be quiet!' She stole back, and positioned herself by the veranda steps with her arms on the balustrade, apparently absorbed in the view.

'Pardon, Mrs. Ribbing, what's become of young Flemming?'

Inés turned, and there in the middle of the veranda stood Konrad, his muscular legs astride. Just then the two German girls arrived and stood beside him, dressed in short, snug riding costumes, carrying little yellow leather whips.

'Flemming,' she said absently. 'I have no idea; he was here a moment ago.'

The young women impatiently slapped at their embroidered leather riding boots with their whips, and Konrad, in a loud irritated voice, shouted 'Arthur, Arthur! Let's get going!'

'Not so loud,' Inés said with a frown. 'You'll wake my husband.' She looked at the man in the rocking chair. 'It's true he's hard of hearing, but even so, there are limits.'

'A fine scandal,' growled Konrad. 'I beg your forgiveness on behalf of my friend, Frøken Mina. Boyish pranks!' With a stiff bow to Inés he left the veranda, followed by the women, their heads indignantly in the air, casting furious sideways glances at Inés.

Inés pressed her hand against her mouth to stifle her laughter, although there was no longer anybody to hear it. Then she tore a twig from the terebinthe tree on the other side of the balustrade and slapped it against her left hand with a pleased smile on her lips. From the courtyard behind the hotel the din and bustle of talk and laughter reached her ears. The donkey drivers shouted shrilly at the animals and cursed in Greek and Turkish, and in among them she could hear Konrad roaring for Arthur. Little by little the racket faded away and finally became a distant hum, mixed with the sound of the donkeys' clip clop.

Inés stole over to the corner of the veranda where the man in the rocking chair still sat unmoving. Then she leaned over the railing to see the procession ride away.

Oh, how beautiful it was here today! Never had she seen the shifting colors so fine and delicate. Or perhaps it was she who saw things differently today? That multitude of hills and terraces, where villas with white façades touched by golden light peeked out from their lush gardens! In the hollows long shadows hung like dull blue gauze over the flowering valleys; here and there hillocks jutted over the water and from their edges luxuriant twining plants tumbled down the steep slopes. The island's brush-covered mountainsides sparkled as if in a rainbow beam, doubly blue as the sun's rays reflected sky and water, and like a saffron-colored ribbon, gravel roads bordered by balsam poplars and pines zigzaged back and forth, far beyond the villas, disappearing amid the dwarf oaks and the blue-green leaves of oleanders—whose clean scent she thought she was able to smell—all the way up to the top, where the little Greek monastery was enveloped in a light white haze. There the travelers came into view high above the hotel and the corner of its wide terrace, which for a few moments had hidden them from her view. They rode two by two, each pair followed by the tireless, lightly-clad donkey drivers. Some young Greek women in colorful national costumes stood along the edge of the path and nodded to them; the procession became longer and longer until the ones in the front began to disappear behind a conical, cypress-covered hill.

'Yes, it's delightful here,' Inés whispered with a dreamy smile, stretching out her arms as if she wanted to embrace the air. 'And you are delightful too, and people are delightful, delightfully absurd.' She took a couple of quick steps, then stopped suddenly, turned and approached the sleeping man in the rocking chair. Stealthily she bent over him and now the smile disappeared. Immediately afterward she straightened up with a short sigh and carefully moved away. She entered the dining room and passed through an adjoining room out to the *karnap* where Flemming stood with crossed arms leaning against a column.

'There, now they're away and we're safe,' she said cheerfully. 'Come on, we'll go down to the grotto.' She placed a white flat-crowned bonnet on her ebony curls, grabbed a parasol and gloves from a mosaic table and walked, followed by Flemming, out onto the veranda.

'The back way.' She nodded her head toward the little gate at the end of the veranda's side wing. Through this they emerged into the littered courtyard, where a tangle of balsam poplars combined their pungent scent with the reek of kitchen garbage that lay in heaps, mingled with the disregarded filth of dogs and chickens.

Flemming was silent and self-conscious, and Inés thought: 'Lord knows how we're going to amuse ourselves.'

'You aren't sorry you stayed home?' she asked in English as she walked along, casting a glance at him over her shoulder.

'Madam thinks I'm a much idiot?' Flemming answered in such wretched English that Inés burst out laughing.

'Just speak Swedish,' she said. 'I understand every word you say, although I can't express myself fluently in that language.'

'I am the same in English,' Flemming remarked.

'As long as you know French — that's the main language in Constantinople among civilized people like us.'

They had come out of the courtyard and were beginning to climb down a narrow, steeply sloping path between the hotel terrace and a sheer embankment, where irregular stones formed a kind of staircase. Inés walked in front. She used her parasol for support and sometimes had to hold out her arms so as not to lose her balance.

'You go in front, Flemming,' Inés said, pressing herself sideways up against the earthen hillside.

Flemming leaned forward, planted his stick firmly between the stones, and in one agile leap was past her.

'There. Take this hand, then I can use the other to steady myself with the parasol.'

'Now I'm as sure-footed as up on the veranda,' Inés said with satisfaction, hopping quickly from stone to stone, led by Flemming. But suddenly she slipped and would have fallen if Flemming hadn't grabbed her around the waist.

'Yes, this is dangerous,' she said and stood still for a moment, leaning against Flemming and catching her breath. Then she freed herself, took his hand again, and soon they were down by the sea where the grotto was a couple of yards from the beach.

'Isn't it wonderful here,' Inés exclaimed, when they had walked into the grotto with its smooth walls of wavy-grained marble and taken a seat on a stone bench in its depths. 'We're sitting here locked up inside the mountain and have no need for the outside world. Imagine if there was a door, a huge marble block that we could close and nobody could open it from the outside. Locked inside a mountain for a thousand years! Imagine if fairy tales were true.'

Flemming sat looking at her from the side. He took a soft, tremulous breath and said nothing.

'I believe the thought scares you,' Inés said, turning toward him.

'Your cheeks are rather green, but I'm sure mine are too. It's the light here inside the grotto. But you can relax, we won't be locked inside a mountain. That could only happen if there was an earthquake. What would you do then?'

'Lie down at your feet and not move from the spot.'

She was surprised by the fervent tone of his voice and it caused a quick feeling of pleasure within her. 'You wouldn't have time for that,' she said, shaking her head. 'We'd be whirled in the air and crushed before we knew it.'

'All the better,' he mumbled.

'Shh! Isn't that somebody swimming? I thought everyone had gone on the tour,' she stood up and walked outside.

Flemming followed.

A couple of hundred yards to the left of the grotto were the brightly-colored bath tents right down in the lapping waves and, some distance out, figures were swimming. The water was calm and clear so that the shapes of their bodies under their thin bathing costumes were clearly visible.

'That's Fru Ruder with her children,' said Inés. 'Do you see how she looks like a crocodile in the water? Of course she's much too prudish to sit on a donkey. And I think her husband is glad she's not along. She's frightfully ugly, don't you think?'

'I've never paid any attention to what she looks like,' Flemming answered.

'Yes but she is. And spiteful, terribly spiteful! Like all these Greek Orthodox women. She hates me and gossips about me. It's just because of my looks. Perhaps you don't believe she gossips about me?' she continued, when Flemming said nothing.

'Yes, but what of it?'

'What of it? What of it?' Inés said heatedly. 'If you hear something bad about me, something really ugly and hateful, then she's the one who said it. You mustn't believe it.'

'That wouldn't occur to me.'

'Come on, before she swims back. Otherwise she'll make a nice story out of this.' Inés hurried toward the grotto, but reconsidered and turned back.

'Absolutely not,' she said with a stubborn toss of her head. 'I'm going to show I don't pay any attention to her. Give me your arm and we'll walk together right by her brown vulture's beak.'

They walked first in the direction of the bath tents, then back along the beach as far as the island's landing pier, which jutted out over the water.

'Just look around you,' Inés said, standing quietly with her arm in his. 'You are walking along so calmly and aren't the slightest bit enchanted '

'I am enchanted,' Flemming said softly.

'What kind of magic is this,' Inés thought. 'It's as if I'm seeing everything today for the first time. That's how it was earlier, too, up on the veranda.'

'Look at the water,' she continued aloud. 'It glitters like gold on azure, and below it's as clear and transparent as the air itself. The little islands over there, look at the way the outcroppings and trees are mirrored; it's as lifelike as if they'd been sliced across the middle and attached at the waterline, one half reaching upward and the other down. And the green is even greener down in the water.'

'Yes,' Flemming said. 'It's beautiful here.'

'Even those ramshackle huts have something idyllic about them, it must be the light.' Inés pointed upward to where a couple of hundred yards from the beach, right below the island's lowest terrace, there was a cluster of little multicolored houses belonging to the donkey drivers, fishmongers and fruit sellers. 'One could wish to live there all one's life. Don't you think?'

'Well, that would depend,' Flemming said.

'Depend on what?'

'Who one is with.'

'Yes, of course.'

'Tell me about your attacks,' Inés began as they were walking back the way they had come.

'Attacks?' Flemming's eyes opened wide. 'Oh, his stupid nonsense! He says things like that to be amusing.'

'Really?' Inés said happily. 'Well you don't seem the type either. So there's really nothing to it?'

'Nothing at all.'

'Why is he so protective and patronizing toward you?'

Flemming blushed to his hairline. 'That's just to impress you,' he said sheepishly.

'Kindly tell him from me that I don't find it amusing.'

'He's quite different when we're alone,' Flemming said with a slight tremor in his voice. 'Now he's grown worse because you call him 'Konrad'.'

'But isn't that his name?'

'Yes, but his family name is Averding.'

'How could I know that? You call him Konrad, and he calls you Flemming, young Flemming, and that is your family name.'

'That's also just when you're around. He wants to pass for older than me, although he's actually a few months younger.'

They continued a moment further in silence. Then Inés asked, 'Do you really like him?'

'Yes, I mean I haven't known him very long — just on the trip. You know I came by way of London and met him on the ship.'

'I'm glad,' Ines said, 'that it's you instead of him who'll be in our office. Come, let's go to the grotto again. We've done enough for Fru Ruder.'

'Are you interested in banking?' Inés asked when they had seated themselves in the grotto.

'No.'

'Why did you apply for the position then?'

'It was my father, or to be exact, my uncle, who knew Herr von Ribbing in the past. Nobody consulted me, and I didn't care.'

'But weren't you something before, I mean didn't you do anything?'

'No. I was a law student, but I didn't really do that either.'

'But now, are you glad you came?'

'I don't really know what my situation will be or what kind of work they'll give me to do.'

Inés felt disappointed by his answer. 'Well, your holiday will be over soon,' she said indifferently.

'Yes, in three days,' he said sadly.

'Is it true what Averding said, that you've never been in love?' she asked with a sudden change in her voice. 'One would think you were weighed down by an unhappy love affair.'

'It is true, I've never been in love.'

'Then why are you so—well, so old for your years?'

'I suppose it's because I'm bored with life.'

'What kind of talk is that?'

'It's not talk. I've always been bored with life,' Flemming said quietly. 'And I thought other people were too, no matter how much they pretended they weren't.'

'There was a period of time when I thought the same,' Inés said thoughtfully, as if speaking to herself; and a little later she added, 'How did you come to a conclusion like that? There are so many happy people in the world.'

'Perhaps. Then I just haven't met them.'

'That's strange!' Inés's tone became livelier. 'Not even children and young people? Children are happy, aren't they?'

'I don't think so. Both I and my peers were very sad in our own ways. As far as that goes—this business about childhood being the happiest age is just something adults try to make themselves and their children believe.'

'Did you have a particularly difficult childhood?' Inés asked, more and more interested.

'No, just the opposite. My parents were well-to-do and showed every consideration toward us children.'

'And even so — I don't understand that. Weren't your parents happy together?'

'They didn't seem to be. My father was bored with his practice, dissatisfied with everything around him, and bitter because he hadn't been made Director of the Royal Hospital. And my mother — poor thing — wasn't happy either,' Flemming sighed.

'What was the problem with her?' Inés said quickly.

'I suppose she fretted over Father, who was so irritable and always falling out with people.'

'Do you have brothers and sisters?'

'Yes, two sisters who had anemia and were always so irritable whenever I talked to them that I realized they must be very unhappy, too, just like I was.'

'The family must have been miserable,' Inés observed reflectively.

'I also have two brothers,' Flemming continued. 'One wanted to be an artist and became mentally ill when he realized he wasn't any good at it, and the other, who's studying medicine, claims he's ruined his life by not becoming a soldier. And that's the way it is with all my relatives, and not just my relatives, but all the people I've known well.'

'Yes, some little thing will always be in the way,' Inés said in a contemplative tone, thinking: 'He's absolutely right. You've always said and thought exactly the same thing.'

'Yes, but this little thing is in the way for everybody,'

Flemming said decisively. 'Precisely the little thing that keeps people from being happy. I've thought about it a great deal. I can almost say that it's the only thing I've really thought about.'

'But take yourself,' Inés began, after a moment's consideration, 'strong and healthy, young and handsome, with good connections and a future that is open before you?'

'But what good is that?' Flemming shrugged his shoulders.

'Don't you enjoy travelling? Weren't you fascinated when you came to Constantinople?'

'Yes. But now that I've looked around a bit, I don't enjoy it any more.'

'Is there really nothing that can make you happy?'

'Yes. When I'm drunk I'm always happy.'

'That's awful!'

'I beg your pardon, Frue! I forgot who I was talking to — no I didn't forget, but it's as though I can say anything to you. Highly incorrect, I know.'

'No, not at all. Just tell me. Is it so much fun to be drunk?'

'Yes, because then everything looks different and I feel happy.'

'I really don't know what to say to you. What if you were to turn into a drunkard? It doesn't take very long for that kind of thing to happen, you know.'

'No, I know that. Two of my friends did it in a very short time. One shot himself and the other committed fraud.'

'You talk about the most dreadful things in a way that would make a person think you're not quite right in the head.'

'But I am.'

'Surely you could find some other way to go to the dogs if that's really what you want to do,' Inés replied in exasperation.

'I don't have an aptitude for other ways,' Flemming said apologetically.

'Well then,' Inés said, 'it's good that you're staying here so I can keep an eye on you. You don't have permission to destroy yourself. I will take it very personally.'

Her voice sounded so warm and earnest that it sent a shock through Flemming. Almost frightened, he looked at her and their eyes met.

'That's the truth,' she whispered, extending her hand, tilting her head a little to the side.

Shy and confused, Flemming accepted her hand. His fingers lay inert against hers and there was a strange contorted expression on his face.

'You don't need to look so miserable,' Inés laughed, quickly withdrawing her hand. 'I won't bother you more than is proper.'

'Did you have an old aunt at home in Stockholm whom you used to confide in?' Inés said suddenly with raised eyebrows.

'How could you know that?' Flemming burst out in astonishment.

'Oh, it was just a thought,' she said casually, getting up. 'But now I can tell from the sun that it's getting late. It's time to go back.' She was already out of the grotto.

Flemming suddenly felt as if a cold hand had touched his heart. Dumbfounded, he sat for a moment reflecting on what had happened there. Then he jumped up and was soon beside Inés who had started the climb up on her own.

'Thanks, but I don't need your help,' she said curtly. 'It's easier going up. Stay as long as you like,' her tone was dismissive, almost peremptory.

Flemming stood still, took off his hat and bowed. Without thinking, Inés turned her head and nodded. She caught a glimpse of his distressed face with its odd questioning look. And as she continued upward, she thought for a second about running back and consoling him, the way one comforts a child.

# II

When Inés walked into her sitting room from the *karnap* her husband was pacing the floor. He turned his back, hands clasped under his frockcoat, so that the coat-tails appeared to be covering a large hump. There was an old man's rigidity about his figure, the long thin legs, narrow sloping shoulders, and angular head that was flat at the back, with straw-colored hair poking out like hog bristles. His dress was fashionable and meticulous.

Inés crossed the floor with her usual light and springy gait. When she had nearly reached her husband, he turned his head and stood still.

'Ah, so there she is! Dare I ask where milady has been keeping herself?' His voice was high-pitched and grating.

'In the grotto,' she answered; she was about to continue but stopped when her husband slammed his heel to the floor with an irritated, 'What did you say?'

'In the grotto,' she shouted, holding her hands up to her mouth like a megaphone.

'Hush, dammit!' He looked at her with an indignant expression in his pale red-rimmed eyes. 'You know I hear perfectly well if you just look at me when you speak.'

She paused for a moment, then gripped the door latch and was about to open it.

'Wait a second, milady! Where are you going?'

'To dress for dinner.'

'Of course! You can't neglect your finery and your toilette. That goes without saying — a lady with so many men chasing after her.' His voice was simultaneously threatening and aggrieved. 'I don't see you all day long — nobody would think I'm the one you're married to.'

'You call this married,' Inés muttered, a scornful smile creasing the corners of her mouth.

'What did you say?' Von Ribbing put two fingers behind his large earlobe and bent it forward so the wrinkles around the corners of his eyes and the narrow ridge of his nose were pulled into greater prominence.

'I didn't say anything. Your ears must be ringing.'

He clapped his hands to his head. 'Satan,' he hissed and two red spots appeared on his sallow cheeks.

Inés turned her head to hide her smile.

'Of course my ears are ringing.' He dropped his hands and shook his little wizened head. 'But who's to blame for that? I say you do it to spite me!'

'What do I do to spite you?' Inés asked innocently.

'As if you didn't know — I always have pain and ringing in my ears if I sleep too long outdoors.'

'But I didn't ask you to do that.'

'What did you say?' He thrust his chin forward angrily and yanked at his earlobe again.

'You're always so angry when your sleep is interrupted!' she called out to him in a loud voice.

'Will you stop that!' He took a quick step closer to her and threatened with his pointed, crooked index finger. 'Tomorrow we're leaving.'

'Yes, of course, it's Monday,' she said in a friendly voice. 'I'm staying here for the rest of the week.'

'We, do you hear! We are leaving tomorrow.'

'No, my dear, I won't hear of it. I have six more sea baths; I must have them. Perhaps you can come and fetch me on Sunday.'

'Thank you very much!' He hurriedly spun on his heel, breathing heavily as he took little steps across the room. Then he came back, stopped in front of Inés and said, 'Now listen, be reasonable. We have our beautiful, airy place in the country. I can come out to you in the evenings there. It's not like here where it's noon before I can be back in the city.'

Inés narrowed her dark sparkling eyes and looked at him warily.

'You know I would be the most loving, the most devoted husband,' he went on with a hesitant glance, 'if you would only let me. Oh Inés, shake off these unworthy admirers. Move out to Therapia and show the world that you have a husband who worships you.'

'Will he never tire of playing this comedy for himself and me,' Inés thought, regarding him with detachment. 'What goes on inside the man's head, anyway?'

'When the season starts in Therapia, I'll move out there,' she said curtly, 'not before.'

'Then can't you just stay in Constantinople until then,' he whimpered imploringly. 'I would have thought you'd had enough of being here at the hotel, with every Tom, Dick, and Harry running in and out. You are compromising me.'

'He must be getting used to that by now,' Inés muttered indifferently.

'What did you say?'

'You can always stay here and keep an eye on me,' she said aloud, looking at him defiantly.

'Thank you very much!' Again he turned on his heel and took quick little steps across the room with the same labored breathing as before.

'And let the office manage itself?' he asked, short of breath, when he returned. 'That would be a wonderful state of affairs!'

'Well, the poor fool has to say that,' Inés thought. 'If he admitted to himself and others that aside from his money he's a nonentity there as well...'

'I suppose you want me to hand it over to Ruder,' he continued angrily. 'Thank you very much! If it wasn't out of pity I would have sacked him as partner long ago. Everything has to go through my hands. Everything, I say.'

'Ruder is no doubt aware of that,' she said softly. And then more loudly added: 'You could let Ruder go on vacation for a while so he could be out here with his wife and children. He would certainly appreciate that.'

'So you could have one more paramour,' he said with a piercing look.

'He works hard all year long,' Inés continued unperturbed.

'Works hard! Did you say works hard?' came the shrill reply. 'You heard me—I'm the one who does the work.'

'Then it's necessary for you to leave. That's clear.'

'And you, too,' he said angrily. 'People talk about us. They think I'm a cuckold. I can tell; I see it in their expressions when they meet me.'

Inés's face was cold and rigid when she answered.

'In that case it makes no difference whether I stay or go. There are many wives here whose husbands only come on Saturdays. Fru Ruder, for example.'

'She has her children! But a woman like you. You don't even have a child,' he hurled the words scornfully at her.

'Would you really want me to have one?' she looked at him with wide mocking eyes.

'You know that very well, my dear,' he said in a sugary tone. 'Haven't I often suggested to you that we take my natural child into our home?'

'Yours!' Inés laughed, a short dry laugh.

'Yes, exactly, mine,' he trembled with indignation.

'Yes, nature plays tricks,' Inés replied, with an airy toss of her head. 'The child as dark as a Turk, and parents white as Cretans.'

He stammered some indecipherable words, lifted his foot and slammed it to the floor so violently that the light wicker furniture shook.

'Now you really must excuse me,' Inés said. 'Otherwise I'll be late for dinner.' And with a curtsy to her husband, she disappeared through the door.

'Bloody Hell! Married to a woman like that.' Von Ribbing spat on the floor and resumed his pacing back and forth.

# III

In the evening Flemming and Averding were sitting together on the veranda. It was mild and still, and the full moon rising slowly over Constantinople's distant heights cast a white shimmering beam of light over the Sea of Marmara. Some of the hotel guests, Inés among them, had been rowed out on the water, some had resumed the game of lawn-tennis they had begun after tea on the terrace behind the hotel, and some had retired for the night, fatigued after their riding tour to the monastery.

Fru Ruder came out onto the veranda with a hat on her head and a full-length cloak wrapped around her tall sturdy figure. She asked the men if they had seen her husband.

'I think he was with the group that went out on the water with Fru von Ribbing,' Averding answered.

'I can't believe that,' she said, almost combatively. 'He promised to wait for me for an evening walk.' She went over to the marble staircase and called loudly for her husband several times.

'If you want to walk, Frue, my friend Flemming here will be glad to oblige. He just said he needs to stretch his legs.'

Annoyed, Flemming poked Averding in the side.

'It would be a pity for your friend to have to walk with me,' Fru Ruder spoke in her habitual tired and whining tone as she approached. 'What in the world would the young man find to talk to me about? If I fancied I could speak Swedish…' she cleared her throat scornfully, 'like Fru von Ribbing, but I don't make myself out to be something I'm not, even though I'm married to a Swede myself.'

'Won't you sit down, Frue?' Averding pulled out a chair.

Fru Ruder sat down in the moonlight, her crossed arms

tightly wrapped in the folds of her cloak. Her raised eyebrows and long sharp nose gave her dark-complexioned face an anxious expression.

'Ah yes, when you're the mother of four children, you have to renounce pleasures,' she said querulously.

'Doesn't Fru von Ribbing have children?' asked Averding.

'Madonna save us! What would someone like her do with children?'

'How old can she be?'

'Exactly as old as I am!' came the gloating reply. 'You shouldn't be fooled by the way she carries on and dresses like a twenty-year-old.'

'Yes, it's difficult to detect age in beautiful women,' Averding remarked.

'Ah yes—beauty...' Fru Ruder drew the word out.

'Men think so,' said Averding.

'Of course,' Fru Ruder laughed scornfully. 'But do you think there is one among them who would want to be married to her?'

'Why not? But as it happens, she has a husband.'

'Yes, von Ribbing, poor thing.' Fru Ruder shook her head sympathetically.

'People talk about him so strangely,' Averding said.

Fru Ruder shrugged her shoulders. 'His wife makes him a laughing-stock.'

'Is it true that he has a harem in Galata?' Again Fru Ruder shrugged her shoulders, and this time she didn't say anything.

'I've heard even worse things about him,' Averding went on, 'things I can't mention.'

'He's been extremely good to us,' Fru Ruder observed. 'My husband is his partner and we owe a great deal to him. If only he weren't married to that Spanish Levantine tart.'

'She's actually a cultured and well-informed person.'

'She's not well-informed, nor cultured, nor does she have proper morals,' asserted Fru Ruder in a tone filled with disdain. 'But that goes without saying, she's Roman Catholic as well. I despise that religion with its immoral priesthood. Now the Greek church! It has more sense because it gives priests permission to marry.'

'You shouldn't be taken in by all the languages she speaks,' Fru Ruder continued quickly as Averding was about to say something. 'We have to do that here. My eldest daughter can already express herself in seven, and she's only ten years old.'

'Do the von Ribbings maintain a large house in Constantinople?' Averding asked.

'Yes, but none of us Greek women go to her balls and parties during the winter. She wouldn't get us if she begged us on bended knee.'

There was a pause. Fru Ruder tossed her head, and a malicious smile appeared on the straight line of her thin lips.

'Are you asleep, Arthur?' Averding suddenly turned toward Flemming who was leaning back on the bench with a burned-out cigarette between his fingers.

'Your friend isn't about to say the wrong thing,' Fru Ruder remarked dryly, then immediately afterward addressed herself to Flemming.

'I'm telling you for your own good, watch out for Fru von Ribbing. Let us look after you. My husband will also be your employer, and in our house you don't risk that kind of thing. You're welcome as often as you wish, and we have—' Fru Ruder suddenly broke off. The faint sound of a child crying reached them from the hotel. 'Oh no, he's awake again,' she rose hurriedly. 'And that Rosalie! God knows why anybody has a nursemaid.' She walked, still talking, across the veranda and disappeared into the shadows.

'Well Arthur, what do you say to that?'

'That poisonous shrew,' Flemming said angrily.

'There must be something to it,' Averding considered.

Flemming didn't answer.

'But perhaps you've already come to an understanding with her,' Averding ventured.

'Oh, leave me in peace.' Flemming said heatedly.

'First tell me all about it.'

'All about it?'

'Surely you don't mean to tell me she wasn't the one who kept you from going on the tour. Play games with the others

33

as much as you like, but you don't fool me.'

'I told you it wasn't her.'

'Oh yes, whatever you say. But you really must excuse me if I warn you.'

'Now you're warning me too?' Flemming exclaimed impatiently. 'I'd have thought it was enough from her — the wife.'

'I promised your father I'd look after you, when he was saying goodbye to you on the ship in London, and I intend to do that as long as we're together.'

'He asked you to do that?' Flemming asked curtly.

'Yes.'

'Then he must have changed his mind when he got back to Sweden, because he wrote from there to say I shouldn't let you lead me astray.'

'Empty phrases,' Averding said disdainfully. 'You must have seen for yourself what a child you are when I was showing you around London.'

'Pah!' Flemming said, striking a match to light a new cigarette.

'You must at least take care to control yourself a bit,' Averding continued amiably. 'You mustn't always be wherever she is, and — '

'I'll follow your example,' Flemming interrupted sarcastically. 'Of course you're never where she is.'

'Oh dammit, she's just so amusing!'

'My opinion exactly,' Flemming said ironically.

'And don't create a scandal like this afternoon,' Averding continued. 'Not showing up for a tour when you've invited a woman to go. If I had been that young woman's brother I would have challenged you.'

'I would have challenged you,' he repeated harshly when Flemming didn't answer.

'Are you quite finished?'

'And now this evening,' Averding went on angrily, 'weren't you about to run down to the water after her when I stopped you? And do you think there's anyone who doesn't see the state you're in? It was a damned mistake to come out here.'

Flemming felt a moment of surprise at Averding's vehemence. 'You were the one who suggested it,' he said, sinking back into his thoughts.

'Yes, like I suggested we should see all the other places around here. But have you been willing to move from the spot? We haven't even been to Skutari!'

'You can go if you want. You'd have plenty of company any day.'

'Yes, you'd like that,' Averding said caustically. 'No thanks, my friend, I'm not abandoning you before I deliver you to the office of Ribbing & Co. And damn them for not taking you right away. You've had enough of a holiday in my opinion.' He stood up. 'Aren't you going to bed?'

'No, not yet.'

'Well, I'm not either.' Averding whistled as he walked down the veranda steps and took the path down to the water.

'The state I'm in,' Flemming thought. 'Yes, what is the state I'm in?' He sighed deeply and looked up at the shining distant sky as he thought about Inés, the way she'd been in the grotto.

If only he could figure it out — oh, it pained him that he couldn't understand why she had suddenly changed down there. And now she was out in the boat with the others while he sat here suffering. He smoked one cigarette after another and the moon rose higher and higher in the sky. Now it was right over the hotel. My goodness, they were staying out a long time.

Suddenly he heard talk and laughter and got to his feet with a start. He recognized Inés's voice and leaned over the veranda balustrade. It was really amazing how the sound carried. He would have guessed they were close by.

'Tired of life?' he whispered suddenly.

'What an idiot! I haven't understood anything at all.' He hid his face in his hands and a slight tremor ran through his body.

# IV

Inés was returning from her morning sea bath. She was wearing a colorful muslin robe with wide sleeves and a sailor collar; her hair was covered with a white lace scarf. In one hand she held an open scarlet parasol and in the other a yellow walking stick. Halfway up the gravel path that led uphill to the hotel terrace she stooped and looked down through the tall trunks of the acacia trees at the water, where the steamer that ran between Constantinople and the Princes' Islands had just pushed off from land.

'Oh thank God, he's gone now.'

She stood for a while looking at the greenish-white, bubbling strip of foam that the steamer left behind on the shiny blue water; then she slowly walked on, her eyes fixed on the walking stick, which she jabbed down into the reddish-yellow sand with every step.

Yes, this was who she was. Now she could enjoy life from one hour to the next. She smiled and shook her head. Someone else in her position would probably have consoled herself with lovers or travelled to Paris and become a court-esan like Madame de Humbert. But dear God, as long as she could avoid seeing him, or at least being alone with him. — It was like having a mouse in the parlor.

Still, if the worst were to happen she would rather have behaved like Madame de Humbert than Mrs. Hobson, who divorced. A woman raised in the true faith—the marriage could not be dissolved. The ones who did would remain in purgatory much longer in retribution.

She had reached the veranda steps, where she paused with one foot on the bottom step and her head bowed, her eyes fastened on the pale yellow buckle of her shoe.

'What if he tried to force me, like he did in the beginning.' She jerked suddenly as if she had been stabbed. 'Pump life into a corpse with the heat of one's body—ah, awful, awful, disgusting!' She pulled herself together, ran up the staircase and was soon in her room, dressing for breakfast.

Time was passing so slowly today. Again and again she fell into a reverie about her husband and her marriage. What was happening? She had finished with all that long ago and he left her in peace. The scenes he made at regular intervals like the one yesterday didn't bother her any more; she either laughed or didn't hear what he said. Had she dreamed of him last night, or was she going to be punished because she had forgotten to say her rosary before going to bed?

Dreamed? No, it was about Flemming, of course, that she had dreamed, that poor Northerner who was afraid she would seduce him. She laughed a little. He must be a philistine at heart, or else he was stupid. Both probably. Strange that she should feel attracted to someone like him—but now that was over, too.

She stuck a gold hairpin into the black curls on the crown of her head and smiled at herself in the mirror. 'Yes, I know it very well. You are lovely, my girl, lovelier than ever, even though you're over thirty. If you want, you can have a lover on every finger. But you don't want that. We agree on that, you and I, isn't that right, Inés? We will wait.' She nodded her proud head.

But the wait mustn't be too long, she thought further, as she fastened black velvet bows on the white bodice of her dress, which hugged her firm breasts and slender waist. 'Time is passing. Time is passing,' she repeated several times in a rushed, barely audible voice. Ugh, these conceited fellows. Idiots. No thanks, that wasn't what she wanted: *'Bella Señorita! Madame, je vous adore.'* She wrinkled her nose.

No, it should be someone quite different, someone like young Flemming, for example. Just as respectful and restrained, and still quite different, and older of course — Flemming was a mere child.

He should be so filled with love that his eyes and actions

and his whole being reflected it. No need to speak, only look at her, only look at her the way she desired.

No, it was a dog she had dreamed about last night! A bloody, howling dog that dragged itself through filth and dry dust to her feet and laid its nose on her shoe. She stared thoughtfully straight ahead and a slight shudder ran through her.

But wasn't it...? She was the dog creeping naked through dust and filth to lay her bloody face on the toe of Flemming's shoe. Holy Antonius! She clasped her hands together in horror and her cheeks grew cold. 'Now I remember it, I lifted my head to look at him and met his gaze — exactly the look I have dreamed of seeing in a man's eyes, and then I turned into a mermaid with a long tail that coiled and twisted. And my heart broke with a crack and I died.' She sank back in her chair before the mirror, hid her face in her hands and sobbed soundlessly.

'Fool,' she muttered as she dried her eyes and applied a little powder. 'Just say your rosary at night and you'll be spared such crazy dreams.'

When Inés came down to breakfast a little later, the others were at the table. The men rose and greeted her. The Spaniard leaped up and pulled out her chair with a smile, a bow, and compliments. The women mumbled a good morning, and the two German girls stuck their noses in the air and turned away with an expression that said: a young German girl does not greet that kind of person.

'Your husband was asking for you before he left,' Fru Ruder said in a reproachful tone. She was sitting across from Inés and sent her a searching glance from anxious eyes.

Inés shrugged her shoulders slightly. 'Aren't you mistaken, Frue?' she asked with a concealed smile. 'Wasn't it *your* husband?'

'Mine? I don't know what you mean.' Fru Ruder turned red under her drab complexion.

'We had arranged to meet before he left,' Inés replied casually. 'There was something he was going to take care of for me.'

'He must have forgotten.' Fru Ruder's hands were shaking as she noisily sliced her cutlet into pieces on her plate.

Inés was conversing with her neighbor as she looked around for Flemming and noticed that his chair beside Averding was empty.

'I'll act as if I don't notice, of course,' she thought, but at the same moment the words flew out of her mouth, 'What have you done with your friend, Mr. Averding?'

'He left on the boat to Constantinople.'

'Without saying goodbye!' Inés cried in astonishment.

'He probably thinks that's customary in this country,' Fru Ruder observed sarcastically. 'And anyway why would he say goodbye. We're in a hotel.'

Inés didn't answer. She felt badly upset by Flemming's sudden disappearance and she would have preferred to question Averding immediately, but felt it was beneath her dignity to show that she was curious. And anyhow, what was it to her?

'You still have all the rest of us, Señorita,' the Spaniard said ingratiatingly, and then began to assure her that there was nothing between heaven and earth that they wouldn't undertake to amuse and entertain her. Her other admirers voiced their agreement, and the ladies looked annoyed.

Inés answered with fleeting smiles and monosyllables, then soon grew silent.

As she was eating she thought about whether her husband could have had a hand in it. Perhaps he had told Flemming that they had unexpectedly found work for him in the office — although that was hardly likely. Why him in particular? The only one who hadn't fawned over her — or — a faint smile played for an instant around her lips — Flemming had left because of her — perhaps he was really not as stupid and helpless as he seemed. Nonsense! How could she have such ridiculous ideas. A boy like that — although not simply because he was a boy — there had been young boys too of course — but they were corrupted. With Flemming it was different.

God knows what he really thought of her anyway. Do you

suppose they had already warned him? Ruder would surely do that today on the ship. She thought she could hear his smug voice talking about how flirtatious and unprincipled she was. Well my young friend, we are fellow countrymen and because of your job with us, we're going to see a lot of each other. You are inexperienced and I will gladly teach you. She suddenly laughed aloud and was asked astonished questions about what she found so amusing.

She shook her head and continued her train of thought.

This Ruder, who for two years had worked persistently to make her his lover. Now he was getting his revenge. He and his wife — the two of them. Of course she didn't know any better. In order to quiet his wife's crazed jealousy, he had no doubt made her believe that his role had been like Joseph's with Potiphar's wife. Fine as far as she was concerned. God, how little this mattered to her.

If only Ruder had been successful at calming the wife down completely. But no luck. Perhaps she knew her husband too well and just pretended that she believed him. Why else was she always wherever Inés was? As surely as the sun rose in the east and set in the west, she showed up. Like now when she'd come out to the Princes' Islands — two days later she was there. Just to keep watch.

Ah, thank God breakfast was over now. She was not in the mood today. They exhausted her, these people with their unctuous voices and their eternal flirtatious prattle, and then they were half annoyed because she wasn't sufficiently enraptured by their idiocy.

'A cigarette, Señorita?'

'No thanks, I prefer my own.'

'What shall we do this morning, Madame?'

'Whatever you want. I'm going to my room.'

A simultaneous outburst of regret came from several voices.

'My head isn't up to fresh air today,' Inés said, walking across the room.

'Fallen out of favor!'

'Heavenly Madonna! Completely fallen out of favor!'

'But you must tell us then — how have we offended?'

They pursued her right to the door through which she disappeared, only leaving reluctantly when they heard her turn the key from inside.

Inside her sitting room, Inés rolled down the venetian blind and settled down to smoke in a rocking chair. The door to the glass *karnap* stood open and through it a soft dull light reached her. She softly pushed her foot against the floor and rocked slowly back and forth while regarding the bluish rings of smoke. From the veranda outside she heard them talking and coming and going. Several agreed to walk to Sphinx Hill. Others wanted to row over to Antigoni and Proti; and Fru Ruder called her children to say she was going down to the beach and they should come along to look for conch shells.

Gradually it grew quiet outside. Inés's hand with the cigarette slipped from the chair arm down to her lap and she sank into a light sleep with half-closed eyes.

Suddenly it seemed as if a momentary shadow had fallen across her eyes and there was a creaking noise from the glass door out in the *karnap*.

She sat up and rubbed her hand across her eyes.

No, there was no shadow and no sound from any door. Ugh, how warm and stuffy it was in here.

She rose, rolled up the blind and opened the windows.

In a corner of the veranda Averding was seated, deep in a newspaper.

'You're alone?' Inés called, leaning out of the window.

He let the newspaper fall with a surprised jerk and said, 'I thought you were angry, Frue, and had retired for the rest of the day.'

'Why should I be angry?'

'Because young Flemming left without saying goodbye.'

'Nonsense. It's suffocatingly hot in here. I'm going up to the lawn-tennis terrace. Do you want to come with me?'

Instead of answering he jumped to his feet, flustered.

'Did you notice whether anybody came into the *karnap* while you were sitting there?' Inés asked.

'What do you mean?'

'Nothing. I thought I heard someone. I'm coming right away.' She left the window.

Ten minutes later they were up on the lawn-tennis terrace. Inés was lying with her head on an aircushion in a hammock strung between two old cypress trees, and Averding was sitting on the grass under a tall stone pine with his knees drawn up, pulling on a rope that set the hammock in motion. His large, slightly protruding eyes slid with a deliberate greedy gaze up and down Inés's body.

'Tell me a little about England,' Inés suppressed a yawn. 'Are the women beautiful there?'

'Yes, but the most beautiful one of all, I've seen someplace else.'

'Is it true that people are so hypocritical in England?'

'Yes, on Sundays.'

'Don't swing me so fast. Slow and easy is nicest.'

'Whatever you wish, Frue. Does this suit you?'

'Why did Flemming go to the city today?'

'A remittance came from Sweden and he had to go pick it up.'

'Why didn't you go with him? I thought you were inseparable.'

'It was quite irresponsible of me. God knows if he won't get all turned around when he tries to find his way back down to the steamer leaving from Pera.'

He's coming back then, thought Inés, and was suddenly in the mood to joke with Averding.

'You'll see, he'll get on the Odessa steamer, thinking it's going to the Princes' Islands,' Inés said merrily. 'Then he'll have to be sent back like cargo. Why aren't you laughing when I'm so witty?'

'I don't find it amusing to talk about young Flemming,' Averding answered irritably.

'That's very unfortunate, because I don't find it amusing to talk to you about anything else.'

'You don't mean that, Frue,' Averding said with unruffled calm. 'You're just saying that to make me jealous.'

'I beg your pardon?' Inés raised herself on one elbow and

looked at him. 'My Lord, I think you're flirting with me.'

'You asked me earlier if anybody had gone into your room,' Averding began in a familiar tone. 'I was in there, Frue.'

'So I did see a shadow in front of my eyes!' Inés exclaimed, letting her head fall back on the pillow. 'That was rather impertinent of you, young Averding.'

'But when I saw you were asleep in the rocking chair, I left right away.'

'Extremely thoughtful, I must say. When people are as intimately familiar as we are — now really!'

'I'm passionately in love with you, Frue,' Averding blurted out.

Inés laughed.

'You find that amusing?'

'Yes, enormously. How old are you now?'

'Oh, what does that matter,' Averding mumbled, red-faced. 'But perhaps the lady prefers someone young Flemming's age?'

'Yes, I like him. He doesn't flirt with me at all.'

'No, he's far too bashful for that,' Averding said scornfully.

'You are not a good friend, Señor Averding.'

'To Flemming, that blockhead? I'm bored with him.'

'And jealous of him.'

'Absolutely not. Flemming — that poor fellow. But it amazes me that a woman like you would have such juvenile taste.'

'Well there you are. Reinvent yourself to be like Flemming, and you'll also appeal to women like me.'

'If you keep on talking to me about Flemming, I'm going to leave,' Averding said irritably.

'Now really! That punishment is just too harsh. Tell me, is Flemming coming back this afternoon or not until the evening boat?'

'I don't have the faintest idea,' Averding said. He let go of the rope and stood up. 'Good morning, Frue.' He tipped his hat and prepared to leave.

'No, first you really must help me out of this hammock,' Inés ordered. 'The sun is starting to hurt my eyes and one of my heels is stuck.'

Averding bent over the hammock and took hold of her feet, whose warm high insteps he could feel through her thin stockings.

'Never in my life have I seen such delightful feet,' he said with a whisper, pressing his mouth to her ankle, grasping with his wide full lips.

'What are you doing?' As she wiggled her foot free, it hit his nose.

'You don't like that?' He straightened up, his face bright red, and looked uncertainly at her.

'You are either as naïve as a eunuch or as cunning as an old roué,' she said derisively. 'No, neither,' she added, laughing. 'You're just a big blockhead. Give me that and I can help myself.' She pointed to the yellow walking stick, which was leaning against a tree trunk.

Averding handed her the stick.

Inés sat up and swung her legs out of the hammock, holding her skirt with one hand and using the stick to support herself with the other.

'What if I were to punish you by telling Flemming about your behavior,' she said as they walked side by side across the terrace.

'Would you consider it worth the effort? You must be quite used to men being forward with you,' Averding said in a cold-blooded tone.

She stopped, gasping for air. The warm peachy-gold color disappeared from her cheeks and with clenched teeth she raised the walking stick and hit him in the face.

He tumbled backwards, pale and appalled. Then he clenched his fists with a movement as if he was about to fly at her.

'That is the way a Spanish Senõra deals with an English lout,' she said in a cold haughty voice, her nostrils white and quivering. 'If you're not gone from Prinkipo this evening, I promise that you will be by tomorrow night.' And with a raised hand and dignified posture, she walked past him and descended the terrace slope.

Averding stayed behind, grinding his teeth in fury. He waved his arms and swore. Then he stroked his fingertips down his forehead and nose where the blow had struck and suddenly burst into a flood of bitter tears.

Was it really true? Had he been struck in the face by this insolent woman—he, the son of an English gentleman with a degree from Cambridge. He walked over to the stone pine where he had sat and rocked her, and stretched out full length on the grass under the branches of its large wide crown.

Had he been too forward—oh to hell with it! That's the way you deal with those types. That's what he'd often heard and also experienced. He had made conquests the same way among mature women back home in England—and she, a Spanish Levantine! And on top of that a notorious one. She should have been glad, this middle-aged hussy, that he wanted to do her such an honor. A big, young, healthy, handsome fellow like himself. To hell with that venomous woman.

If he could just find a way to get back at her. He pondered for a long time and envisioned the wildest schemes.

Then he looked at his watch and jerked upright. The steamer was coming soon and he had to leave on it. That devil of a Levantine tart could get her thuggish paramours to assassinate him. At the very least she would make his visit intolerable through harassment and persecution. And anyhow it was below his dignity as an English gentleman to sit at the same table with this woman whose scorn had left a mark on his face. Hurry down and pay and pack his suitcase. Luckily most of his baggage was at the hotel in Constantinople.

A half hour later the steamer docked at the landing pier. Among those disembarking was Flemming.

'Passengers to Proti, Antigoni, and Constantinople!' the mate shouted from the ship in piercing English.

Some colorfully-dressed Greeks who had been clustered around the donkey drivers' huts hurried aboard. After them came several Asian merchants, tall and stout, with broad yellow faces, wearing turbans and silk tunics, and finally a couple of Turks with long beards who walked with measured steps in their baggy trousers and full shiny kaftans, followed by a motley group of children.

'Passengers to Proti, Antigoni, and Constantinople!' the mate repeated his cry.

When Flemming had crossed the gangway and stepped ashore, Averding popped up in front of him.

'Are you leaving?' Flemming asked in surprise.

'Yes,' Averding answered indifferently. 'I'm bored with hanging around here doing nothing and I can't get you to go anywhere with me. Last night you advised me to take off on my own and now I've done it. Goodbye old chap, and thanks for the company.' He grabbed Flemming's hand and shook it.

'Where are you off to?' Flemming asked, not quite recovered from his surprise.

'To the Caucuses and the Himalayan mountains, or maybe to Spitsbergen. You'll hear from me.'

'Passengers to Proti, Antigoni, and Constantinople!' the mate shouted for the third time.

'Fru von Ribbing and I have fallen out,' Averding said with a bitter laugh, hurriedly starting to move. 'I gave her an earful, that's for sure!'

'What's that stripe on your face?' Flemming called after him.

Averding turned, gestured with his hand without slowing down and said something that Flemming couldn't hear.

A moment later Averding was on board. The two friends saluted each other with their hats in a last farewell, as the steamer cast off and backed away.

Flemming opened his white umbrella and started up the hill. In spite of the intense heat he walked with rapid springy steps, all the while tilting his head back and looking attentively up at the hotel terrace.

Suddenly he stopped with a jerk and his heart started to pound so hard he felt it in his back. Inés was coming into view at a turn in the path up the hill.

He drew quick hard breaths and struggled to calm down. If only he could hide someplace so she wouldn't see how lobster-red and flustered he was. If she spoke to him, as she surely would when they were nearer, he would be in no condition to answer. Impossible. He stood there gasping for breath, nearly suffocating.

Scarcely knowing what he was doing, he whirled around and started to run straight back down to the landing pier. There he turned left and walked down the beach toward the bathing tents along the same route he had previously walked with Inés. When he reached the grotto he ducked inside and sat down.

He put his hat down on the stone bench and dried his sweaty face. Blood hammered in his temples and throat, and his heartbeats gradually grew slower.

If he had just stayed in Constantinople! But he'd had no peace there, just rushed to get back. He had wanted to be so bold and confident, talking with her in the same free and easy way as Averding: flirting, paying compliments, and now... What must she think of him? Make fun of him, laugh at him, despise him — what a weakling! Or think he was out of his mind?

Well, he really was out of his mind. He had been ever since yesterday down here in the grotto. Out of his mind with joy. Why?

Because she existed, because she looked at him, talked and smiled at him, was in his presence. Out of his mind with longing that had awakened in his blood, from notions as alluring as enticing dreams, from hope, from intoxicating feelings of joy that suddenly changed to anxiety, pain, and dread.

And now, could he dare hope that she hadn't recognized him back up on the hill! What a ridiculous figure he had cut! But no, she could see very well, could read the name of the steamers when they were passing far away. Oh God, what an unhappy man he was! He leaned back with his burning head supported by the cool stone wall, closed his eyes, and folded his hands on his vest. He felt himself sinking into a well of hopelessness.

A rustling sound caused him to open his eyes. Inés was standing at the entrance to the grotto. Her large dark eyes were laughing at him.

Flemming sprang up like a rocket.

'So this is where you're hiding out, Mr. Runaway,' Inés said in a tone as if she were interrogating him.

'It was so hot outside,' Flemming stammered.

'And so you ran to cool down?' Her friendly tone dispelled Flemming's embarrassment.

He smiled and looked at her gratefully.

'No, but seriously. what came over you?' Inés stepped inside and sat down beside him.

'I really don't know. Sometimes a strange shyness comes over me. Of course you couldn't understand that — '

'When you are tired of life, I suppose?' Inés interrupted, with a roguish smile.

'I was thinking of going back on the evening boat without showing myself at the hotel,' Flemming continued. 'Now that Averding has gone.'

'So he's already left. I didn't know that.'

'He was going on board as I was landing.'

'And without his company, you can't be happy here?' There was a mocking ring in her voice.

'No, but he was always my companion, in a way. Remember I fell out with all the others after the trip to the monastery yesterday.'

'Oh, that's nothing to be worried about,' Inés said indifferently.

'Yes, because I'm so out of place and alone here.' There was a nervous twitch in his eyebrows and the muscles around his mouth. 'All these foreigners I can't talk to. The only one who's been friendly to me is you, Frue.'

'What about the juveniles?'

'Oh them! And anyhow, they hate me now of course.'

'I think the only correct thing to do is to take you completely under my protection, since it's my fault you backed out yesterday. It's only right.'

'Oh, if you would, Frue! You'll be my trump card!'

'I'll keep you occupied from morning to night. Are you happy now?'

'Yes, very happy,' Flemming said with a beaming face.

'And we'll start right away,' Inés continued, rising with a brisk movement. 'Now help me up the stone path. We'll have to go the shortest way because it will be time to eat soon. But remember, people are going to gossip about you.'

# V

One afternoon a few days later, Inés stood in her sitting room with her arms crossed over her chest, lost in thought.

Behind her, the door from the dining room was quietly opened by a negro waiter.

'Ma'am rang?'

Inés turned and waved her hand: 'Never mind,' she said curtly, but before the waiter left she added, 'Ask Herr Flemming to come in for a minute before he leaves.'

'Yes, Ma'am.'

'Through the *karnap*.'

'Yes, Ma'am.'

Inés sat down, stood up again, and walked around the room for a bit. Then she picked up a book and leafed through it.

A couple of minutes passed before she heard Flemming in the *karnap*.

She walked to meet him with the book in her hand.

'I'd rather say goodbye to you here,' she said rapidly, 'because I won't walk you down to the steamer after all. There are so many people.'

He stood before her with dangling arms and downcast eyes; the expression on his pale face resembled the marble cupid with an arrow through his heart in her bedroom at home.

'I've kept the promise I made in the grotto the other day, isn't that right?' Inés asked with a faint smile.

'Yes, Frue,' Flemming stammered out.

'Have you packed?'

'I'm not quite finished.'

'Then you'd better hurry.'

'Yes,' Flemming mumbled.

'Goodbye then, and thank you for spending time with me.' Inés extended her hand to him.

He raised his eyes, took her hand and looked at her, as his trembling lips whispered a soft goodbye.

Inés felt as if she'd received an internal blow. Never had she seen a look so filled with hopeless, submissive pain. She had to wait a bit before she could say in a steady voice, 'We'll meet again soon.' Then she released his hand with a soft squeeze and Flemming left the *karnap*.

Inés stood in the same spot, staring ahead. 'He loves me, he loves me,' a voice inside her said, and it was as if the blood in her body suddenly came alive.

She entered the sitting room and bustled around the room, 'Sweet little Flemming, dear Lord, so upset.'

Suddenly she stood still and a triumphant smile flashed across her face. 'I'll do it, I'll do it,' she whispered, and then looked at her watch. She sprang over and pressed the bell button, then went to the *karnap* to fetch her gloves and hat, which she put on without looking in the mirror.

'Bring me my black cloak. It's hanging in the wardrobe in my room — the long cashmere one, you know,' she said to the waiter who had just come in.

A moment later he was back, helping Inés put on her cloak.

'I have something to take care of in Constantinople,' she said, pushing her hands into the wide Dolman sleeves of fine black lace. 'I'll probably be back around breakfast time tomorrow,' she added, as she was knotting the cloak's silk ties around her neck. Then she grabbed her parasol and hurried off. She took the back way across the rear courtyard, through the gate, and soon was down at the landing pier where the steamer had just arrived. Hurriedly she slipped aboard and took a seat in the corner of the rear bench at the right of the binnacle.

A number of passengers came on board. Inés recognized a few and held her parasol in front of her to avoid greeting them.

But where was Flemming? The steamer's whistle and the

mate's shout had already warned twice about their departure. What if he was late? She peeked under the parasol at the landing pier above and suddenly caught sight of Flemming in the middle of the entrance to the gangway. With a start she moved further back on the bench and lowered the parasol so that her face was completely hidden. Even so, she could clearly see where Flemming was. Toward the middle of the ship he was leaning on the railing with his arms crossed. His head was tipped back, his face turned up toward the hotel terrace. He had placed his suitcase on the deck close by. When the ship had cast off and turned, he moved away, and the cabin on the rear deck hid him from Inés's sight. Soon afterwards it began to get dark.

'In a quarter of an hour it will be quite dark and I'll go and find him,' Inés thought, leaning back on the bench with a long, deep, sigh.

And what then? What did she want with him? This timorous bashful child, so like a young girl?

But he loves me, he loves me and I can't bear to see him suffer. I will make him happy — sweet little Flemming. To have the power to create for someone the greatest bliss or the deepest despair — wasn't that happiness?

But what about the other ones — Averding, Señor André, and Antonius — she could make them happy too. Yes, but not heart-broken, and that was the difference.

She felt happy, so amazingly light and free. It was as if each breath she drew lifted her out of herself, and although she was sitting quite still on the bench, it seemed to her that her whole body was in throbbing, surging movement.

The mate came around selling tickets. When he was standing in front of her he lifted his cap in greeting.

'He recognized me, even though it's dark,' Inés thought. 'Of course, he probably saw me when I came on board.'

The ship, which initially was heading in a northeasterly direction, now changed course and headed due north. Inés turned on the bench and looked back at the Princes' Islands. The air was so pure and clear, and the islands' dark contours were etched sharply against the starlit heavens. Along

Prinkipo's steep mountainside, the lights from the villas were sprinkled like glowing embers, and the Sultan Achmet Hotel looked like an illuminated castle. With a fleeting smile she thought about what they would be saying inside about her sudden disappearance.

When Inés turned back again, she saw a male figure coming astern on the port side and recognized Flemming's easy, nonchalant gait. It struck her that his legs were not very elegant. They curved outward slightly above his knees, and she remembered as well that his feet were a bit too flat. A few feet away from Inés, Flemming stopped and kneeled on the bench that encircled the ship's stern, with his arms over the railing.

'If he had any idea I was sitting here,' Inés thought. And she suddenly wondered why she didn't go over and speak to him. She knew very well that he was staring out toward Prinkipo because he thought she was there. What had become of her joy at the thought that she could make him happy? She was almost at the point of wishing she was back at the hotel.

She was seized by a vague melancholy. A perception of the world's emptiness and vanity swelled within her and she thought that if she had become a nun that time when she was fifteen and disappointed in love, she would now be shut away in a convent, hidden away from the world's sins and sorrows. Suddenly it struck her that the English naval officer she was in love with then resembled Flemming. The same slender height, blond curly hair, beautiful blue eyes, full red mouth, and large pearl-white teeth. And it was on board a ship, a warm starlit evening like this one, that her fate had been determined. She saw before her the polished deck with many lanterns where they danced under a sail canopy. And the ship's lounge that resembled a greenhouse where he had begged for a lock of her hair and she had fallen into his arms and said, 'Yes, yes. Take my hair and me! I will follow you to England.'

The moon was coming up over the hills of Kadikoy and the forest-covered headlands of the Asian coastline, and the light fell with a bluish sheen over the ship's deck. In half an hour they would be across from Leander's Tower and then directly

*Constantinople*, Postcard, undated (ca. 1905)

into the Golden Horn.

Suddenly Flemming turned and sat down on the bench with his back against the railing.

Well, the Princes' Islands must be out of sight now. Inés peeked at him. His face, which was bathed in moonlight, had the same anguished expression as when they said goodbye up in the *karnap*. And again, Inés was flooded with compassion and happiness.

A commotion started up around them now that they were sailing in from the Sea of Marmara. Steamships piped and whistled; from vessels and *caiques* came shouts of *'guarda!'* Aboard the sailing ships loud commands were barked out, and a man in a fez and *stambuline* tramped back and forth on the quarterdeck.

'I'll wait till we're disembarking,' Inés thought. 'Then I can talk to him more freely.'

They had passed Leander's Tower and were now traveling at half speed between the gleaming lights of Skutari's clustered houses and the Seraglio Point, with its jagged line of marble kiosks and black plane trees against the background of Stambul's white minaret towers inside the Golden Horn. The heaving mass of ships' rigging and lanterns were framed by Constantinople's illuminated hills, where houses and palaces, minarets and domes were piled up on the steep slopes and etched against the sky like enormous pyramids.

The engine reversed, the anchor was lowered. The ship swung up against the current and right away they were surrounded by ferrymen loudly calling from their white *caiques*, in various languages, offers to be of service.

When nearly all the passengers were off the ship, Flemming stood up and slowly walked across the deck.

Instantly, Inés was behind him.

'Good evening, Flemming,' she poked her head around the edge of his shoulder.

He turned as if struck by lightning and took a step back. Inés could see his face turn whiter than the moonlight.

'You don't want to go ashore without your suitcase,' she said. 'It's over there. I had a good view of you when you came on board.'

He retrieved his suitcase and again stood in front of Inés, looking as if he was sleepwalking.

'Let's hurry before the ferrymen are gone.' Inés walked ahead and soon they were seated in the *caique*, which was rowed by a young Turk in a turban and open shirt.

'Do you realize that you haven't even said "good evening" to me?' Inés said, her heart pounding with a strange joy.

'I was so surprised to see you,' Flemming mumbled.

'Well, the cat must have your tongue. You haven't even asked why I came over here.'

'I thought you would tell me that,' Flemming answered. He sounded as if he was struggling to speak and his eyes didn't leave Inés's face.

'You really are phlegmatic, aren't you?' Inés said a bit impatiently. 'If I were in your place…'

'I'm still overwhelmed,' Flemming said in the same strained way. 'It feels like a cork has got stuck in my throat. I get that way when something unexpected happens to me,' he added apologetically.

Just at that moment the boat landed at Galata, where the houses extend right down to the waterline and a narrow walkway is used as a landing stage. Flemming paid and sprang ashore with his suitcase, after which he helped Inés up.

They walked silently, side by side, through narrow, dirty, barely illuminated streets of flimsy wooden stalls, shabby cafés, and unsavory lodging houses. Braziers outside the houses sent greasy smoke toward them as they made their way with difficulty through the partly Asian, partly European mass of humanity, and every moment they had to watch out for the wretched cabs and carriages whose emaciated hired horses were driven forward by the whiplashes of the coachmen running alongside.

'We'll take the funicular up,' Inés said, turning into a crooked alley at the end of which they came to a building that lay at the foot of a hill and resembled a truncated tower. From the street they walked directly into a small waiting room where they bought tickets at a booth from a man whose face was

*Constantinople - Quay of Galata*
Postcard, undated ( ca.1914 )

visible behind an open window, and walked from there into a steeply upward-sloping tunnel where a number of flickering gas lamps along the narrow platforms cast a wavering light on the double tracks. There were as usual only a few passengers at this time of evening, and Inés quickly found an empty car, though the entire train consisted of only four cars.

Flemming took a seat across from Inés. His delicate white hands, resting on his knee, were trembling slightly, and his face was glowing with quiet rapture.

'And this is a man who doesn't show his feelings,' Inés thought, turning her head toward the window. She felt his glance like a ray of sun on her face.

There was a shout and whistle from outside, and then came the sound of a winch being turned. The car jerked and with a heavy clatter the train began to work its way up the steep rails.

'It's better for you to sit on this side,' Inés said. 'Otherwise you really have to brace yourself.'

Flemming, who couldn't hear what she said, leaned toward her with a questioning expression.

Instead of answering, Inés seized his head with both hands and kissed him on the mouth.

With a gasp that sounded like a child's long suppressed sob, he collapsed against her, wrapping his arms tightly around her shoulders as he covered her mouth and cheeks with burning silent kisses.

'My sweet little friend, my own sweet friend,' Inés whispered, returning his kisses. Her eyes filled with tears of emotion, feeling herself in the arms of this trembling human being who was giving himself completely.

Just then, a hollow boom roared in their ears and with furious speed the car they were sitting in slid, creaking and groaning, back down the hill. Inés and Flemming closed their eyes and held on to each other tightly. In a couple of seconds the car stopped with an ear-splitting crash and a bump that flung them against the opposite seat, after which they were again lifted up as if by unseen hands and thrown back to their previous places. The car stopped with one end in the air, shuddering as if it was going to break apart, then fell down hard on the rails. The sound of screams and shouting voices reached them; the door of the car was ripped open and a uniformed man ran from car to car asking if anyone was hurt, without waiting for an answer. They heard passengers crawling out onto the platform, cursing and scolding. Some complained that they were badly injured, and everybody talked at once. A loud voice threatened a police investigation. This was the second time in the course of the summer that the cable had broken.

Inés and Flemming sat quite still, leaning back with their hands clasped.

'Are you hurt?' Flemming asked when the commotion had died down.

Inés softly squeezed his hand. 'No, not a bit. How about you?'

'I'm just so dazed, I'm not sure I can stand up.'

'Me too,' Inés touched her head. 'My hat, it's gone.'

'Mine too.' Flemming got up and found both hats on the floor of the car under the seat.

'Well, now we'll have to walk up those odious steps,' Inés said as she put on her hat and straightened her cloak.

'There are two trains now, there was only one before,' Flemming said as they climbed out and crossed the platform.

'Of course. There are always two working at a time; the one that leaves from Pera lifts the one going to Pera. When the cable breaks they both fall down.'

They walked past the man in the booth, who called out to them that they should get their money back, but they hurried on and soon were in the crooked alley.

'This was a bad omen,' Inés said, taking Flemming's arm and holding tight.

'Are you superstitious?' Flemming asked.

'Yes, are you?'

'In any event not when I'm as happy as tonight,' he said in a voice drunk with joy.

'But where are we going?' Inés asked, stopping with a jerk.

'I don't know. I'll go wherever you lead me, even to the

*The Grande Rue De Pera,* 1876

ends of the earth.'

'Ugh, no!' Inés said with a shiver. 'You're talking nonsense. We go this way.' She turned right and there directly in front of them was the hundred-step street slanting steeply uphill, illuminated by occasional gas lanterns, murky light from houseware stalls on both sides, and a narrow shaft of light from the moon that was just peeking up behind the Pera hilltop.

They began to climb slowly up the uneven, worn stone steps, where puffing pedestrians in turbans and Turkish trousers, in Greek national costumes, and in Armenian clerical robes were struggling along among gold-embroidered Albanians and dark-clad Europeans with fezes and questionable women. A couple of reckless horsemen came racing at a gallop on horses ready to drop from fatigue. One of them brushed past Inés so closely that Flemming had to hastily pull her aside so she wouldn't be knocked down. Shortly afterwards she was nudged in the back by some Turkish sedan chair bearers who laconically kept walking, bearing their gilded cage from whose window a veiled woman was peeking.

Finally they came to the end of the steps and turned onto the Grande Rue de Pera. Here there was less traffic. The shops had put out their lights, and in mounds as large as rock piles on a country road dogs had settled for the night on the corners of the small side streets where they made their homes.

'Where are you staying?' Inés asked.

'The Pera Hotel.'

'Yes, but later?'

'Ruder thought I should take full board there.'

'Nonsense. You must see about finding lodging someplace else. Then I'll come visit you.'

Startled, Flemming impetuously squeezed her arm.

'Your suitcase,' Inés burst out, coming to a halt.

'It's on the funicular,' Flemming said, pulling her along with him.

'If only it hasn't been stolen.'

'It doesn't matter.'

'I'm home now.' Inés stopped beside a high wrought-iron gate behind which was an expanse of a park-like garden illuminated by moonlight.

Flemming seized both of her hands and wouldn't release them. 'Why did you come to the city?' he whispered.

'To say goodbye to you one more time.' Smiling, she looked into his eyes.

With a soft rapturous sound he leaned his face toward hers.

'No, not here! Are you out of your mind — kissing me out on the street.'

'Then let me come in with you,' he begged.

She pushed open the wrought iron gate and they walked in.

'Wait here, while I see if von Ribbing is home. In among those trees over there. In case somebody comes.' She walked with light steps down the sloping garden on a white gravel path, past the fountain in the center encircled by tall tropical plants, through an allée of acacias onto a lawn at the bottom of which lay the impressive house. With a single glance Inés saw that all the windows were dark. Hurriedly she walked along the back of the house, with its projecting balcony supported by Ionic columns, all the way down to the corner of the spacious courtyard, which was enclosed by tall trees. Along the back the windows were also dark except for a single light shining on the ground floor. The servants and the Turkish cook lived there.

'No,' Inés said, when she had rejoined Flemming under the trees. 'He must be out or else he's gone to bed.'

Flemming pulled her toward him and kissed her.

'But I still don't know,' Inés said as she gently pushed his face away. 'It's too dangerous to take you up with me. You could meet him when you're leaving.'

'Isn't there a summerhouse where we could sit down?' asked Flemming.

'Yes, just a second.' She led him out of the trees to one of the garden's side pathways and into an arbor with comfortable benches and a low oblong stone table.

When they sat down Flemming threw his arms around her

and overwhelmed her with caresses.

'Let's talk to each other a bit, instead,' Inés said at last, trying to free herself. Aren't you extremely surprised?'

'Surprised — yes, no, about what?' Again he tried to kiss her.

'You're taking all this as if it's an everyday thing,' Inés said with sudden frost in her voice. 'Perhaps you think it is for me?'

Flemming released her. 'Are you angry with me?' he asked, almost afraid.

'No, but I don't like it that you haven't asked me anything.'

'What should I ask you about?'

'That's something you'll have to figure out for yourself.'

Flemming didn't answer. He just sat with his head down.

'Now I have to go.' Inés was about to leave, but Flemming suddenly grabbed her dress to hold her back. Then he slid onto his knees before her, threw his arms around her body and hid his face in her lap with such a violent movement that his hat fell off.

'Your head is so beautiful,' Inés said, running her fingers tenderly through his hair.

He stayed down without moving.

'Get up,' Inés said after a while. 'I have to go in now. Von Ribbing could come back any second.'

'First say you're not angry with me,' Flemming begged with his face raised.

'No, I'm not angry with you.'

'And say you're fond of me.'

Inés took his face in her hands, bent down, and kissed his forehead.

'Do I really have to leave you now? That's dreadful.'

'Yes, but you *must*.'

'First call me "Arthur", just once.'

'Yes Arthur, my dear Arthur. Get up now.'

He stood up slowly without releasing her.

'You want me to call you "Arthur", but have you ever called me "Inés"?'

'Oh Inés, Inés,' he gripped her tightly and lowered his head to her shoulder.

'Early tomorrow I'm going over to Prinkipo Island again. Meet me outside here at 9:30 and you can walk with me to the steamer. You can tell the office that you have an errand to run. No one will mind when you've just started.'

'Outside the wrought-iron gate?'

'Yes. You can walk around a bit if I'm not out there right away.'

'When will I see you again?'

'I'll be back here on Monday, but I can write to you about that. The Pera Hotel then. You write, too.'

After a long and passionate embrace Inés tore herself loose.

'Goodnight, Arthur.'

'Goodnight, Inés.'

Passing through an ornamented gateway and doors that were always left open, Inés entered the hall, ran softly up a broad staircase, and pressed a hidden button that opened the balcony room door. There were white curtains over the windows, but the moonlight shone through the cloth so Inés could find her way without bumping into anything. From the balcony room she walked through two spacious, formally furnished rooms into her bedroom, a deep, oblong room at the back of the house. She found matches on the nightstand, lit the candles in the candelabrum that was attached to a wall covered with pale flowered Persian cashmere beside the dressing table, and took off her cloak.

Glad to have slipped in without anyone in the house having seen or heard her, she collapsed onto a soft chaise-longue, the cover of which, like the bed hangings, was made of the same fabric as was on the walls. Her mouth and cheeks were burning from Flemming's heated kisses, and she could still feel his tender embrace.

It had really happened, she had found a man who loved her in such a way that she wanted to give herself to him. That was what she wanted — with no shadow of doubt or second thoughts. He would have her, have her completely. She closed her eyes and a tremor passed through her at the thought of the joy Flemming was going to experience.

Yes, and she herself too. It must be successful this time.

Why should she be made differently than other women, she with her healthy, vigorous body. She had passion and desire within her, or why else would she feel this mysterious rapture in dreams that she never experienced while awake. But in Flemming's arms — oh, she was sure of it. She would no longer feel herself despised by nature, not be barren and shut out of what was the origin and joy of all life. Stirred by a sweet yearning, her breast heaved with a trembling sigh and tears filled her eyes. Imagine becoming a human being, a complete and authentic human being who for once would feel the joy of life streaming through her, be filled with rapture at being alive.

But what if after all ... An ill-defined doubt welled up in her, and she thought with faint pity about what had happened after a two-year marriage of appearances to von Ribbing, when she let herself be taken by a young French attaché, who all winter had been pining away and courting her. Such a bitter disappointment that had been, when her surrender had brought her nothing, absolutely nothing, neither pleasure nor satisfaction, and then she had abased herself by going on with it, pretending she was happy out of laziness, or shame about revealing her abnormal incapacity; well actually, she herself couldn't really understand the reason, but one thing was certain, the relationship ended solely because he was suddenly called home. The tired and hopeless resignation she felt when she went to bed the night she saw him for the last time. A spent and impossible human being.

And now after — well, how many years had passed — she was sixteen when she married, eighteen when she took her lover — and now after thirteen years had gone by she was awakened again. Well, there were the dreams of course, but never during those years had she felt the slightest attraction towards or feelings for any of the men who approached her. Not until she met Flemming.

But suppose now — oh nonsense. It was impossible. To-night her whole body had trembled with pleasure at his caresses. Although she had also felt the same when the Frenchman kissed and embraced her, *before* she gave herself to him.

Well, the die had been cast. She knew what she wanted, and she was deadly serious about it.

But now she had better see about going to bed.

She got up off the chaise longue and fetched bed linens from the cupboard. As she was making the bed she jumped at the sound of the gate downstairs closing with a bang.

He was coming home. Good thing they hadn't stayed any longer in the garden.

She finished making the bed and began to unbutton her dress. Suddenly she paused and listened anxiously.

Surely he would never — yes, there was no doubt. She heard his short stiff steps approaching from the adjacent room.

Seized by an ill-defined alarm and displeasure she hurriedly blew out the candles.

At that moment he tried the door and then knocked loudly.

'Who is it?' Inés called out and approached the door.

'It's me!' His voice was excited.

'What do you want?'

'Open up, dammit!' He knocked again.

'Tell me what you want from out there. I can hear perfectly well.'

'If you don't open up, I'm going to force the door.' He pounded with a clenched fist.

Inés turned the key and opened the door.

He rushed into the room, a lighted lamp in his trembling hand, and looked around with a rapacious expression in his small bloodshot eyes.

Inés, who had stepped aside, watched with a scornful face as von Ribbing walked around the room, illuminating it with the lantern.

'Are you looking for something?' she asked in a loud voice.

'I'm doing what I please,' he answered angrily, continuing his rounds. In front of the bed with its embroidered silk bed-spread and fine lace-trimmed sheets turned back, he stood still for a moment. Then he kicked his big foot under it from every direction, and setting down the lamp, ducked down with difficulty and peered under it.

Inés continued to watch him.

When he was upright again with the lamp in his hand, she walked over and threw open the doors of the large closets.

'And this,' she said, hurrying over to the chaise longue and giving it a shove with her hand that sent it rolling across the floor.

'Do you think you are conducting yourself properly?' Von Ribbing spoke louder than usual to hide his disappointment. 'Coming home in the dead of night without my knowledge and sneaking into the house like a thief.

'You do nothing but spite and compromise me! I have to endure having my servant come whispering to me in confidence that there is a light on in madam's room.'

'Call him your spy instead,' Inés said calmly.

'What did you say?'

'Nothing.'

'Yes, I've certainly been a fortunate man.' His agitated tone gave way to a peevish whimper. 'Do you think these are the thanks you owe me because I covered your father's debts and provided you with a life of luxury and comfort?'

Inés smiled coldly.

'But of course,' he laughed bitterly, 'you can't pick flowers out of a dungheap. Your origins are much too common for anyone to expect you to have either honorable feelings or a conscience.'

'Can't you save the rest of this until morning?' Inés said with a yawn. 'I'm so tired tonight.'

'Why did you come to the city?' von Ribbing shouted. 'I will know that, do you understand!'

'It's really quite simple,' Inés answered, shoving the chaise-longue back into place. 'I'm going to my dressmaker early tomorrow to try on dresses.'

'Spending money like crazy! Always the same. Wasteful, wanton, squandering,' he uttered, jerking his head at each word. 'Besides, you're lying of course.' He sounded crestfallen and stood for a moment lost in thought. Then he clenched his fist, swung a thin arm toward her and said, 'But you watch out. Just watch out. I will catch you and then — .' He turned suddenly and walked toward the door, but immediately rushed back and whispered hoarsely, 'If I ever catch you, I'll have charges brought against you as a common whore. Just so you know.'

'Of course,' Inés said in her friendliest tone. 'What else would you do?'

'Of course,' von Ribbing snarled, breathing heavily. 'You just wait. I'll bring you to heel.' A second later he was gone.

Inés closed the door after him, undressed calmly and went to bed.

# VI

When the servant brought tea up to Inés the next morning, a letter was on the tray. Although she had never seen Flemming's handwriting, she knew instantly the letter was from him. She opened it immediately and with a happy, eager expression began to read the three short pages of delicate sprawling letters with inch-wide spaces between the lines and words:

Dear Inés!
I am so overjoyed tonight that I can't go to bed before I've told you that. My window is open and the music and singing from the vile tavern in the garden across the street doesn't bother me in the least, which it otherwise would have done. Quite the opposite, I almost think listening to it is enjoyable. I think I'll stay up as long as it goes on, but then I'll smoke too many cigarettes. Thank God I don't have to drink like I did before to drive away my boredom.
I look forward to tomorrow when I'll see you, and it's been a long time since I've had anything to look forward to, so long that I can't even remember when.
Your sincerely devoted,
Arthur

With a disappointed expression, Inés let the letter fall into her lap. She sat for a moment sunk in deep thought, her face toward the window from which she could see the Galata Tower with its glass gallery and little conical roof and, a bit to the left, the towering Suleman Mosque with its domes and four minarets crowned by green hills. She shook her head a couple of times and muttered, 'your sincerely devoted — your sincerely devoted — oh, that man!'

Suddenly she stood up with a hurried movement and, snatching a box of matches from the nightstand, went over to the black marble heating stove in the corner, pushed the letter in and set it afire. Afterwards she calmly finished her interrupted toilette.

An hour later she walked through the garden's gilded wrought-iron gate and turned left onto the street without looking around.

It was Friday, the Muslim Sunday, and the crowds were so great on the narrow crooked street that Inés could only with difficulty make her way.

Lines of carriages escorted by *kava'er*, and filled with children and veiled women who were out to make purchases in the Greek and French shops, had to drive at walking pace in order not to run into each other. Sedan-chair bearers continuously shouting *Guarda!* pushed carelessly against anyone in their way. Horses and oxen pulling loaded carts forced themselves through throngs of corpulent eunuchs; solemn, turban-clad Turks; tall thin Armenian priests with their white square caps and black veils, Turkish civil servants in fez and *stambuline*, and European pedestrians of every nationality. Beggers resembling bundles of rags sat huddled together outside houses; dogs rooted around in refuse heaps that reeked under the sun's powerful rays, and street hawkers called out their wares in every possible language. Small shopkeepers had moved their stalls inside gateways, and greengrocers had strung up their wares against the houses and on the hinges of street doors.

Struggling to inch her way forward, Inés berated herself for not saying yes when the servant asked if the horses should be hitched to the carriage. It was up to Flemming to watch the time and realize she had given up the idea of meeting him. But he wasn't there anyhow, the blockhead!

'Good morning, Inés!'

Inés, who had stepped aside to allow the passage of a little man with no legs who was humping along on his hands, quickly turned her head and saw Flemming beside her.

*Pera, Constantinople*
Postcard, undated

'So there you are,' she said indifferently. 'I thought you had forgotten.'

'I suddenly caught sight of Averding and ducked into a doorway,' Flemming answered breathlessly.

'So he's still here.'

'And he shouldn't see me walking up to meet you, should he?'

Inés shrugged her shoulders. She had started walking again. Flemming tried to stay by her side but it was almost impossible.

'I'm going in here,' Inés said, stopping suddenly outside a Roman Catholic chapel. 'Goodbye.'

Flemming flinched as if from a blow and gave her a frightened look. It was clear that he had only now noticed her coldness. 'I don't want you to walk me to the ship after all,' Inés said brusquely, turning the shaft of her parasol. 'What happened last night was completely reckless on my part. The car we were riding in must have been bewitched. Besides it's just too dangerous. Von Ribbing must have gotten wind that something was wrong. Last night he came in and searched my room. I want to get out of this...' she broke off, still turning the shaft of her parasol.

Flemming stood there biting his bottom lip, with his cheeks flaming red, smiling uncertainly. 'You don't mean that,' he said. His smile had given way to trembling lips when Inés lifted her eyes to look at him.

'Yes, I mean it,' Inés nodded vigorously. 'How can you presume to believe...' She turned around and disappeared through the chapel door.

Flemming stared after her, as motionless as if turned to stone. One arm was raised, the fingers outstretched as if he was clutching at something. Then he was bumped in the back by the muzzle of a horse, pulled himself together, and stumbled back the way he had come.

When Inés walked into the chapel, she devoutly made the sign of the cross and dabbed herself with holy water from the marble font by the entrance. She bought a votive candle from an acolite, lit it, and carrying it in her hand walked up the flagged stone floor between two rows of prayer benches, past the large crucifix in the center, where she again crossed herself, then over to a side altar behind which a wax Virgin Mary, with uplifted hands and a gold halo around her head, was standing in a niche surrounded by wreaths and a jumble of burning votive candles.

Placing her candle on the altar, in a candle-stand draped with orange and blue glass beads, Inés turned away after crossing herself for the third time, slipped into a pew, kneeled down and mumbled a string of Latin prayers, thinking of Flemming with disappointment and aversion. As she was reciting the prayer to the Virgin Mary to keep her mind and deeds chaste and pure, she felt a moment of contrition, but promised herself that when she got home from Prinkipo, she would immediately go to confession and get absolution.

After ten minutes had gone by, she stood up, walked lightly and calmly out of the chapel, and a few hours later, was at the Sultan Achmet Hotel with her admirers, with whom she made an excursion in the afternoon. That night when she went to bed the experience with Flemming only seemed halfway real to her.

But the next morning the post brought a letter from Flemming, splotched with tears that here and there blotted the handwriting. It read like this:

Dear Inés!
Although I fear you don't want this, I'm writing to you any-way. I must, I know I can't do otherwise. I've been sitting locked up in my room all day without moving, without eating. When you left me, I went home and wrote to the office that I was sick. And that is true. I am sick, I am out of my mind, I don't know anything, I can't remember anything. It had been dark a long time before it occurred to me to light the lamp. I haven't smoked one cigarette, I've had no desire to drink. When a person is full of either joy or sorrow he has no need to get drunk. It's just the boredom that makes that necessary. I've learned that now.
Oh, Inés, Inés, don't take my sorrow away from me the way

you've taken away my joy. Let me hear from you and see you from time to time. Hear you say you will not let me be with you like this morning, not have anything to do with me any more, so my sorrow can remain fresh and free me from emptiness.

What have you done to me, Inés? And what is my offense toward you that you want to hurt me so? Why did you let me live this way for the past five days if you wanted to destroy me afterwards? Since that first time in the grotto, I've been alive—before that I didn't know what life was.

Does it make you angry that I call you '*du*'? I can't help it. I can't do anything, I don't know anything—everything has gone dark around me. I weep, just weep.

Let no one ever know the feelings I've nourished for you and unfortunately still nourish; that would be the same as blasphemy. And I swear to you that on my side what has happened between us will be an eternal secret.

Yours until death, faithfully,

Arthur

Inés answered:

My own dear Arthur!

Your letter has made me sad and happy. Forgive me for the way I treated you this morning. But how could I know it would upset you so. You just stood there smiling, and from the letter you sent me yesterday morning, I got the impression that you took the whole thing as a casual amusement or an everyday event and I didn't like that. I wanted you to be quite otherwise, filled with amazement, more captivated and confused than you seemed to be. I didn't like it either when you wrote 'your sincerely devoted, Arthur.' It sounds so bourgeois and stiff. But now I can see that you have a strange way of expressing yourself, or more accurately, that you can't express what you feel. So I will love you in spite of that.

Now you must be happy again, my dear boy, and go nicely to the office if you haven't been there today. Meet me on

Monday at the Bosporus Park. You know the public park that you come to after you pass Taxim barracks at the end of the Grande Rue de Pera. Between 12:00 and 1:00. It's lunch time and you'll be free from the office. Then we'll eat together in the restaurant and I'll find a chance to kiss you into happiness again.

Your,

Inés

To this letter, Inés received the same evening a short thank-you note that was composed of calm and boring expressions. But now she didn't let it upset her mood. She immediately put it away in her writing desk and once again began to read through the letter from the morning.

# VII

Inés and Arthur were sitting together in Bosporus Park on the terrace in front of the open-sided restaurant pavilion. They were finished with lunch and the waiter had cleared the table. Now he came with coffee and liqueurs.

'Now you'll see their eyes get big over there,' Inés said, taking out her cigarette case. 'I beg your pardon, *meine Herrschaften.* I intend to smoke.' She glanced mockingly at a party of German men and women who, with enthusiastic torrents of '*famos*' and '*wunderschön*,' were looking through binoculars at the delightful view over the Bosporus, its azure water surrounded by heavily gilded white and pink marble palaces, the mosques and gardens and green-clad heights sparkling and gleaming in the brilliant sunshine.

'Aren't you going to smoke?'

'No,' Flemming said, 'I'd rather look at you.'

Inés smiled tenderly at him and squeezed his hand under the table.

Suddenly a surprised expression came over her face. 'Look behind you,' she said quickly.

Flemming, who was sitting with his back to the garden entrance, turned his head and immediately turned back to Inés.

'Our beloved juveniles,' Inés said. 'I must say, we are lucky. As soon as we make the slightest move, something terrible happens.'

'Should I greet them?' Flemming asked.

'Of course, as soon as they come up on the terrace.'

Shortly afterwards the two German girls, accompanied by an elderly gentleman, brushed past the table where Arthur and Inés were sitting. Flemming lifted his hat and the two young ladies acknowledged his greeting with an almost imperceptible nod.

'The only one missing was Averding,' Flemming said, beaming with enjoyment.

'That's right,' Inés sighed, 'Averding is here as well. Do you see how many dangers we're surrounded by already?'

'Yes, but he wasn't with them,' Flemming answered cheerfully.

'But what if they run into him now? Of course they'll meet him. The first thing they'll do is tell him they saw us together. He'll immediately go to Ruder with it. You can be sure he'll be hanging around the Ruders once Mommy gets home.'

'Well, just let him.'

'Easy for you to say,' Inés said, slightly miffed. 'You don't have a wife who is Ruder's partner, nor an enemy named Ruder.'

Flemming looked as if he didn't understand.

'What did Ruder say about me on the steamer?' Inés asked suddenly.

'I don't remember.'

'So I was an object of discussion?'

'Yes.'

'I knew it!' Inés burst out, 'and I also know what he said, that sneak. But you're not listening at all to what I'm saying. Why are you staring at me like that?'

'Because you are so lovely,' Flemming took a deep breath.

'Do you think Averding is still here?'

'It's not impossible.'

'If you meet him, you must tell me everything he says about me, do you hear? Every word.'

Flemming nodded.

'But come on, let's leave. We can hardly hear ourselves speak over these loud Germans.'

Flemming tapped his glass and paid the waiter, who came over right away.

As they walked out of the garden Inés took a coin out of her purse and handed it to Flemming.

'What should I do with that?' he asked, flushing with

*Therapia on the Bosphorus*, 1905

embarrassment.

'Now listen, Arthur! In this domain we are comrades, nothing else. Don't you think I can afford to pay for the food I eat?'

'But it's too much,' Flemming muttered.

'Oh well, then we'll use the rest another time. So it's settled that we pay our own way when we're out together.'

'When we're out together,' echoed inside Flemming, and a feeling of intoxicating happiness flowed through him.

'You still have a good half hour free,' Inés looked at her watch. 'This way, and I'll show you a quiet place.'

They walked past the massive Taxim barracks with its impressive entryway and soon afterward into the sprawling cemetery that lay behind it, with its hundred-year-old cypresses and endless rows of low headstones that, without any earthen mounds, marked the Turkish graves.

Flemming took Inés's hand and slipped it through his arm; his face was turned toward her and he gazed down at her intently.

'Can you hear the silence?' Inés said and stopped.

Flemming lifted her hand to his lips and kissed it.

Inés lifted her mouth to him. He threw his arms around her and walked backwards with her in his arms to a tall, narrow headstone that was topped with a turban. He leaned back against it in a nearly sitting position and pulled Inés down on his knees.

Inés put her arms around his neck and pressed kiss after kiss on his mouth.

'You're going to drop me,' she finally said with a laugh, sliding off his trembling knees. 'Come, let's walk around a bit.' She stood upright in front of him.

He wanted to pull her back to him.

'No, it's much too creepy here, with all these skulls and skeletons. She shivered and suddenly looked pale. 'It's horrible in these Turkish cemeteries where you're walking around on skeletons. They bury their dead just under the surface.'

'You've gotten so serious,' Flemming said when they were again wandering arm in arm under the mighty trees.

'Well, it was stupid for us to come in here. This is no place for people like us.'

'All places are equally good as long as you are there, Inés.'

'I can't stop thinking that soon I'm going to be under the earth as well—cold and mute in the terrible, eternal peace,' Inés said.

'That won't be for a while,' Flemming said cheerfully and squeezed her arm.

'Even if I lived to be a hundred years old, that's still not very far off. Just the fact that death exists turns even the longest life into nothing.'

Flemming didn't answer. He was much too happy to be infected by her mood.

A little while later Inés said, 'All these signs that keep haunting us. First the funicular, then the juveniles, and now this. Yes, because the fact that the two of us happened to walk into the cemetery is also a bad omen.'

'Oh, you and your omens and your superstitions. As far as that goes, dying isn't the worst thing. I would gladly lie under the earth here if I could share the grave with you, Inés.' There was such a sincere and convincing ring to his voice that Inés was moved and whispered, 'You darling.'

'But it couldn't be here,' she then added. 'I've bought a grave plot over in Skutari that a Roman prelate blessed when he was here two years ago.'

'And people think you are worldly,' Flemming said teasingly. 'You are more like a nun.'

'It is the most charming Catholic cemetery,' Inés continued. 'Like the one we had back home in Alexandria, that's why I loved it right away. It's near the Bosporus on three hills covered with shady, sheltering groves. Where my grave plot is located you can hear the soft lapping of the Bosporus waves as they roll against the mossy wall that surrounds the cemetery. It sounds like sighing and like an endless lament.'

They had come to the end of the cemetery, where a wide and open roadway led straight down to the Bosporus. Now they turned and walked back by way of a side path.

'You're letting me do all the talking,' Inés said. 'The only time you really talked was down in the grotto.'

*Turkish woman in cemetery at Skutari opposite Constantinople*
Photograph, 1909 -1919

'I don't think I need to talk,' Flemming answered. 'I have a feeling that you look inside me and know everything I think.'

'Do you remember that I asked you then if you had an old auntie at home you used to confide in?'

'Yes. Why did you get so strange all of a sudden?'

'You don't understand, you stupid boy?' Inés squeezed his fingers.

'No, I didn't and don't understand. What does that have to do with you?'

'You'll get a kiss for that.'

She stood on tiptoe and pressed her lips to his cheek.

'But explain it to me.'

'All right, but some other time. You are so sweet, Arthur.'

'We'd better go our separate ways here,' Inés said when they came out of the cemetery. 'I'm going to visit the wife of the English Legation secretary. Then I can say I was there for lunch if I'm asked about it.'

'When can I see you again?' Flemming asked, holding tightly to her hand.

'I really don't know. Meeting in the street like this is so dangerous.'

'Well you could.. ' Flemming's whole face reddened as his trembling fingers squeezed her slender hand.

'Could what?'

'It's nothing. I'll write to you about it.'

'You mean, let you come home with me?'

'No, absolutely not. But I'm — do you remember you said I should find other lodgings? It's done, Inés.'

'And for that you're looking like you committed a crime?' Inés laughed.

Flemming expelled a deep breath in relief, and his face glowed with grateful joy as he said, 'It's Smyrna Street, Number 11, a little two-story house. The landlady is a German widow who lives upstairs and I've rented the downstairs rooms.'

'That's wonderful, my dear!'

'Will you come tomorrow?'

'Yes, although no, not tomorrow,' Inés said, looking a bit

flustered, 'but in a few days, as soon as I can.'

'Oh, please! Come tomorrow. Regardless, I'll be standing at the window from ten after twelve and until I have to go back to the office.'

'Well, perhaps. But I can't stay very long.'

'Thank you, Inés.'

They looked into each other's eyes, a long deep gaze. Then walked in different directions.

That evening after tea time Inés was sitting in her room thinking about Flemming. She really had not believed he had such initiative in him. Imagine possessing and controlling a person so completely! She would also make him happy in return. Her cheeks flushed and blood coursed warmly through her.

'When shall we go to Therapia?' Von Ribbing had come into the room.

Inés grabbed a straw hat and began to poke artificial flowers into it.

'After the French opera has been here,' she said in a loud friendly voice.

'That means in about two or three weeks?'

'Yes, approximately.'

'Then you'll speak with the gardener and the servant about what needs to be done?'

'Naturally.'

'As far as I'm concerned it makes no difference whether we're here or there,' von Ribbing said crossly. 'But since one does own a place in the countryside... I suppose young Flemming should be invited to stay out there for a week or so?'

Inés pricked her finger and dropped the hat so it slid to the floor. Von Ribbing, standing a step away, bent over to get it. Inés bent over as well and their heads collided.

'I'm sorry,' Inés said, flustered, and with a 'thank you', took the hat from von Ribbing's hand.

'You see, I can be just as attentive as any of your admirers,' von Ribbing said with a faint smile, touching his hand to his head, which had a red spot after the bump. 'One is, after all, a gentleman, thank God. But back to young Flemming — otherwise Ruder will invite him and I don't want that. That guy always wants to make himself important and get there first. But it's me, not him who is a friend of Flemming's uncle, and it wasn't to him but to me that Flemming was referred. Am I not right?'

'Of course you're right,' Inés answered.

'He'll only be there at night, so you wouldn't be bothered,' von Ribbing said with a piercing look. 'Naturally he'll come to the city with me in the morning, and we'll come as usual at 7:00 for dinner. Incidentally, there is certainly no making a businessman of him. He's too unpunctual, the blockhead.'

'Already?' said Inés. 'That's hardly an auspicious beginning.'

'Well, I'm off now. I'm going to meet a business friend at Café Paris.'

'That means, I'm going to my little girlfriends in Galata,' Inés said to herself.

Over at the door, von Ribbing turned and, with a satisfied expression, said, 'Do you see how well I hear when you just speak clearly? I didn't make you repeat a single thing.'

Inés threw her hat on the table when von Ribbing was gone and leaned back in her chair with a thoughtful expression.

At length she said aloud: 'We'll have to be careful then.'

# VIII

The following day Flemming was standing behind the sheer curtain of his window on Smyrna Street peering out. His head was hot and blood was pulsing in the veins of his temples.

The rectangular room had a double window, a low ceiling, and was covered with shiny gilt wallpaper. There were Biblical oleographs on the walls, and a beaded carnation basket filled with straw and soiled paper flowers hung from the center of the ceiling. The furniture was made of pearwood and consisted of a sofa, coffee table, corner cupboard filled with German knick-knacks and topped with a cracked pointed mirror, a writing desk, console mirror and spindly wooden chairs—all in the European style. The only things suggesting Turkey were the carpets on the floor and table and a wide, long divan in Persian colors with massive round pillows, in front of which stood an inlaid octagonal table, quite battered and low to the floor. There were two doors, one that led to an empty little vestibule with coat hooks on the wall and the other to the bedroom.

Flemming looked at his watch. He tucked it back into his vest pocket, but then took it out again, unhooked it from the chain and placed it on the windowsill. It was a quarter to one and he was supposed to be at the office at one thirty. She wasn't coming.

A little later he walked out to the vestibule and closed the red mousseline curtains in front of the low small-paned window.

Then he returned and resumed his post.

Just then he caught sight of Inés part way up the street and with a start he fell back into the room. But a moment later his face was again pressed against the windowpane.

93

Inés was walking down quickly with her parasol on her shoulder. Occasionally she turned her head rapidly from side to side.

Flemming moved silently out to the vestibule, where he listened for a moment at the door. Then he went out into the narrow dark passageway with its steep bare staircase to the second floor and opened the street door halfway.

A moment later Inés slipped in. Without a word she walked past him through the vestibule into the next room where she released the curtain holders and pulled the curtains across the windows, so they were completely covered.

'You don't need to be afraid,' Flemming said, following her. 'I've been standing by the window for three quarters of an hour and not even a cat has walked by.'

'It's a perfect spot. The end of a blind alley and that long black plank fence instead of neighbors. How in the world did you find it? I'm impressed by how ingenious you are.' Beaming, she held out both hands to him, and Flemming rapturously pulled her to him.

'It smells like patchouli and old cigarette smoke,' Inés said, twisting out of his arms. 'I'll have to see about bringing some decent perfume in here.' She pulled off her gloves and loosened her coat of ivory lace underlaid with dark red satin. 'God knows what kind of people lived here before. A couple of criminals like us, no doubt.'

'But really this is perfectly satisfactory, and hideous through and through,' Inés said, looking at the walls and faded carpets. 'But that doesn't matter when the location is so good.' She was in front of the mirror adjusting the lacework on her low-cut, cream-colored dress.

Flemming threw his arms around her from behind and kissed her tawny neck.

'I've spoken to Averding,' he said.

Inés turned around quickly and gave him a questioning look.

'He didn't say anything that would interest you,' Flemming continued. 'He'd made a couple of excursions in Asia Minor—he talked a lot about that—to and from Constantinople. Today he's going to Crimea and Odessa, and then he'll be back only one more time before travelling home.'

'He didn't mention me?'

'Yes he did. He wanted to know how things were between us, but I feigned indifference so well that he got the impression that the subject bored me and stopped asking me questions.'

'Who would believe you could be so artful,' Inés tugged his earlobes and fell into a reverie. Several times it had been on the tip of her tongue to tell Flemming about the scene with Averding, but embarrassment about telling him that a man like Averding had dared to insult her had held back her words. The same was true now.

'Well, just watch out for Averding,' she said with a nod. 'I'm certain he would do what he could to make trouble for us.'

Flemming led her to the divan, where he sat down and pulled her to him.

'Not so hard,' Inés said. 'Your kisses are smothering me.'

Flemming immediately released her and buried his face in her lap with a deep sigh.

'It's terribly warm in here,' Inés said after a bit. 'And you're getting my dress so wrinkled people will be able to see I've come from a tryst.'

Flemming didn't move.

'Get up, Arthur! I *have* to go now. That's why I didn't want to come today. Next time I'll stay longer.'

Flemming instantly obeyed and stood in front of Inés, gazing at her with a sick expression.

'And I thought you would be glad I came,' Inés said reproachfully. 'You look like I've injured you.'

'No, no, Inés, I am so very happy. I love you, oh, I love you,' he took out his handkerchief and wiped his face with it.

'When will you come again, Inés?' he asked imploringly, when she was getting ready to leave.

'As soon as I can.'

'Tomorrow?'

'No, not tomorrow.'

'What am I going to do tomorrow? I can't bear it, Inés. Can't

I come visit you?'

Inés considered it. 'No,' she said, shaking her head. 'He has set his trusted servant to keep watch on me—I can feel it. And besides—no, I don't want to see you until the next time in this room. I'll write to you.' She spoke in a tender, secretive tone that made Flemming's blood race straight to his heart.

'All right, whatever you want,' he whispered back.

She put her arms around his neck and kissed him. Then she tore herself loose and left.

Theodosia Kaufmann

Midwife

Night bell on the left

Inés glanced unthinkingly at the sign on a door as she turned the corner of the last house on Smyrna Street and entered the Pangalti Quarter.

'God knows what a creature like that looks like,' Inés thought a little later. 'That anyone would dare trust her life to an ignorant woman when there are doctors available.'

When Flemming came home the following evening from a restaurant dinner with Ruder, he found a letter from Inés announcing that she would come the next day.

He blew out the lamp, threw himself on the divan, and pressed the letter to his lips. He lay there, senseless, intoxicated, as hours passed like minutes. When he got up to go to bed the day was already dawning.

In the bedroom he pulled up the venetian blinds before lying down. And with the letter in his hand and his eyes fastened on Inés's thin, stiff strokes, which letter by letter were imprinted on his brain, he lay without feeling sleepy or tired, his cheeks warm and his eyes shiny with tears, until the landlady banged on his door from the outer room and said that the tea tray was there.

'Well, here I am.' As on the previous occasion, Inés came immediately into the room after Flemming had opened the door and now stood in front of him with outstretched arms, her head slightly tilted and a dazzling gleam in her coal-black eyes.

'No, stop, let me do it myself,' Inés said, as Flemming, after a long embrace, was tugging at the ribbons of her hat. She undid the little bow by her ear and laid her hat on the table. Then she took off her coat and stood there with downcast eyes and bowed head. Her slim fingers plucked nervously at the bows on her dress and her breast rose and fell rapidly under the thin lace fabric.

Flemming came over to her, took her hand and kissed it for a long time. Then he grabbed her by the waist and pulled her to the divan. Inés hid her face against his chest as they slipped with their arms entwined down onto the soft bed.

# IX

Inés was home, sitting in the arbor of her garden on the Grande Rue de Pera. In her hand was an open book, which she wasn't reading. Her eyes had a tense expression, and every few minutes she would start and listen.

Then she heard the garden gate open. She got up from the bench, peeked out, caught sight of Flemming and softly called out to him.

'My God, are you sick?' Inés said, when Flemming had stepped under the dense foliage of the arbor.

'I was awake all night in despair because you didn't come yesterday,' Flemming said, leaning against the arbor's foliage. 'You promised you would come.'

Inés looked away with an annoyed expression.

'Make me almost insane with happiness — and then afterwards … But I could tell when you left me the day before yesterday. You looked so peculiar. That's why I had to write to you right away.'

Inés tossed her head. She pressed her lips together and turned her head even further away.

'And then the letter I got this morning,' Flemming continued in a dry, flat tone. 'It was so cold and distant.'

'Well, I was very annoyed with you,' Inés blurted.

'I thought as much,' Flemming mumbled.

'Absolutely not for the reason you think,' Inés said almost angrily, and turned her head toward him. 'I should regard myself as being seduced by you? Are you out of your mind? Me! Have I not given myself to you freely and honestly, and you write that I mustn't believe you are one of those men who cared for me less because you had gotten what you wanted. My God! How disgusting!' She stood up abruptly and immediately sat down again.

Flemming, who had turned quite pale, looked at her with a devastated expression.

'And you think I value myself so little,' Inés continued with a trace of scorn in her voice.

A flaming blush shot rapidly up into Flemming's face and on his slim white throat. He stood with confused eyes, looking as if he could sink into the earth.

Inés was seized with compassion. 'Don't you understand how that would offend me?' she asked, mildly reproachful.

Flemming wanted to answer, but he couldn't get the words out. He bit his lower lip, as if he was on the verge of tears.

Inés got up, walked over to him and put her hands on his shoulders. 'You mustn't take this so hard, Arthur,' she said. 'I won't scold you ever again. It's wrong.'

He pressed his face against her throat and wept quietly.

'Now, now, my own dear Arthur.' Inés kissed his cheek and patted his hair. 'You mustn't cry, do you hear, Arthur?'

Flemming lifted his head and dried his face.

'You are so high-minded, Inés, and I'm so ashamed and small,' he whispered in a tearful voice. 'Through you I get to see into a new world and become new myself. I suddenly understand what freedom means. Freedom to love, and suffer, and die. Almighty God! This makes life holy, and you are holy, Inés , and I become holy through you.' He slid down against her dress, but Inés pulled him up and put her arms around him.

'I love you, Arthur! From now on, I'll love you precisely because you are the way you are. I wouldn't have you any other way, not for anything on earth.'

'Oh Inés, if you can just bear with me. If you can just take me as I am and look away from the disappointments I understand I cause you—I'm the one who receives everything and gives nothing,' he implored humbly.

'You give me yourself completely, more completely than any other person could. That's the greatest happiness.'

A bit later, Inés said, 'But now our time must be up. '

'I'm not going to the office today. We have the day free.'

'Really!' Inés exclaimed happily. 'Well, I'm also free for the rest of the day. Von Ribbing is going around with the officers. He's not coming home for lunch or for dinner either. Today they'll dine with the Swedish Minister and tomorrow at one of the pashas.'

'God makes miracles for us,' Flemming said. His face glowed as if lit by the sun.

'Yes, isn't that true! That the corvette came now instead of before we met. It's been expected for ages. But listen, you got yourself a ticket to the French Opera tonight, didn't you? Because now, of course, von Ribbing has made our box available to the Swedish officers, so there won't be a seat for you.'

'So we can be together right until we go to the theater?' Inés nodded.

'And every day between twelve and one you'll come to me?'

'Yes, as long as the corvette is here. Later on we'll have to find another time, because I can't always be away for lunch, you know. But we'll worry about that when the time comes.'

'And now are we are going off to our den of iniquity?'

'Together? No, you've gotten too bold.'

'Well, separately, then.'

'No, come up with me instead. Louis, the servant, you know, is out driving with von Ribbing and the officers, so we can be fairly safe. Now I'm going up first and you come right after. Up the stairs and through the door straight ahead. It will be open.' She nodded and disappeared.

'Here is my territory,' Inés said, when Flemming had come through the balcony room into the two spacious rooms behind which Inés's bedroom lay. 'On the other side of the balcony room are von Ribbing's rooms, and down below are the dining room and our other rooms for entertaining. You'll see the ballroom sometime, it's much more beautiful than your Swedish Minister's. We'll probably have a party for the corvette and you'll be invited of course.'

'No, you really must prevent that,' Flemming said.

'Why is that?'

'I couldn't bear seeing you in the company of so many admirers, while I don't dare speak to you.'

'Yes, but think about knowing that you and I understand each other with just one glance, that we have a secret that no one suspects, and that invisibly binds us in the midst of all the others. You shall come.'

'All right, if you insist.'

They settled down on the low corner sofa wrapped tightly in each other's arms. Inés's head lay on Flemming's shoulder.

'Don't you ever get tired of kissing me?' she whispered at last.

Flemming lifted his head and looked at her with eyes that shone with delight. 'No, never, never,' he whispered back and buried his face in her velvety throat.

'Shush,' Inés whispered suddenly. 'Isn't somebody coming?'

Flemming listened for a moment. 'There's nothing,' he said, pulling her closer to him.

'Yes there is!' Inés burst out anxiously. 'Let me go!'

'Who would be coming?' Flemming mumbled in an intoxicated voice. 'It couldn't be von Ribbing anyway.'

'For God's sake, let me go!' Inés wrenched herself upright. 'Do you hear, he's in the next room! Let go of me, we're lost!' Inés had torn herself free with a powerful effort. Her face was pale grey and her whole body was trembling.

Terrified, Flemming jumped up. Now he could clearly hear the approaching footsteps.

'Hide! Hide! Oh God! Oh God! In there.' She pointed to the door of the bedroom.

'There isn't time!' Quick as a flash Flemming ducked down behind the grand piano in the center of the room, whose legs were hidden by a loveseat.

Just then the door opened and von Ribbing crossed the threshold in a full-length tan duster and with his hat in his hand.

'So there you are,' he said to Inés, who was standing with her back turned, fiddling with a rubber plant on the floor in front of the piano. Her knees were shaking and she could barely hold herself upright.

'It's disgraceful how poorly Jean takes care of the plants,' she said loudly and breathlessly as she hurriedly walked past von Ribbing into the next room, through the door her husband had left open, where she pretended to press the bell button.

'What's the hurry?' Von Ribbing followed her. 'Can't you give me one minute?'

Inés turned halfway toward him and put her hand on her forehead.

'I have a terrible headache,' she said and groaned.

'And I'm in a terrible hurry,' von Ribbing said importantly in his dry raspy voice. 'I'm on my way to an audience with the Sultan, with the Minister and the Swedes, and the day after tomorrow I'm having a dinner for them. That was what I wanted to tell you The corvette sails already on Saturday. They've postponed the ball until after they return from the Black Sea, so no need to order your ball gown quite yet.'

'I was not at all certain I would even be going,' Inés remarked.

'What did you say You have to make the necessary arrangements with the cook The Minister is coming, and all the pashas — forty place settings. I have to invite Ruder, of course — and that fellow, Flemming. Tell the cook not to scrimp, plenty of champagne and the appropriate wine with every course.' He put on his hat and hurried to the door.

'How will I get to the opera tonight?' cried Inés, who had now completely regained her composure.

'The carriage will be home in time to take you. We'll come afterwards. I'll instruct the coachman to fetch us at the Minister's residence after he's driven you to the theater.'

Inés waited for a bit. Then she slipped out to the hallway and peeked through the large bay window into the garden, where von Ribbing was just disappearing into the acacia allée. When she heard the garden gate slam shut she returned to her boudoir and with a searching glance positioned herself where her husband had been standing.

'No, you are very well hidden,' she exclaimed, as she moved around a little, squatted down and with her hands on the floor peeked under the grand piano where Flemming was crouched on all fours.

'But imagine if he had come around to this side,' whispered Flemming, staring at Inés in terror.

'Isn't it terrible how danger follows us. Whatever we do, the evil omens continue to haunt us.'

'Except in Smyrna Street,' said Flemming.

'Oh, just wait,' Inés mumbled and fell into a reverie.

'But dear God!' Inés began to laugh. 'Are we going to lie here eyeing each other like a couple of kittens,' she stood up, still laughing.

Flemming stood up as well and straightened his clothes.

'Think of behaving in such a comical way,' Inés said, throwing herself into an armchair and bursting into laughter again.

Flemming looked at her for a moment. Then he was infected by her laughter and they both laughed until tears ran down their cheeks.

'Oh no, no, I can't any more,' Inés dried her eyes, but right away started laughing again.

Finally Inés managed to get her hilarity under control.

'It's from fear and excitement,' she said, exhausted. '*Les extrèmes se touchent comme toujours.*'

'Yes, it was a terrible moment,' Flemming said, suddenly growing serious.

'We can't do this again,' Inés burst out. 'You *must not* accept the invitation to stay with us in Therapia. Something disastrous would almost certainly happen there,' she said, staring straight ahead, with an expression of fatigue and distaste on her face that Flemming had never seen before. He glanced anxiously at her.

'What are you thinking about?' he asked after a moment.

'That what I'm doing with you is utterly reckless,' Inés answered darkly, without looking at him.

A spasm of pain crossed Flemming's face.

'You don't realize what I'm exposing myself to,' Inés began in a tired, dead voice. 'You haven't a clue about my relationship with von Ribbing or how he would react —

you're also a strange person,' she broke into an irritated tone, 'anybody else in your position would have wanted to know about that right away. But look at him and see if he cares.'

'When I have you, Inés, and you are good to me, I don't care about anything else in the world,' Flemming said humbly. 'Everything else is so unimportant that I forget it exists.'

'Yes, but what about me! Is it also unimportant to you how I am, why I am an unfaithful wife, and what happens to me?'

'Now you're already forgetting that you promised to love me just the way I am.'

'You haven't even asked me if I live with my husband the way other wives do,' Inés continued impatiently. 'What do you really think about me?' She shifted her eyes to him and met his confused, unhappy glance.

'Oh, now I have it!' Inés cried, jumping to her feet. 'You've just accepted the gossipy stories you've heard.'

Flemming shook his head.

'Now for once you *are* going to speak out,' Inés stamped her foot on the floor. 'I want to know what you feel and think.'

'Inés, how can you treat me like this?' Flemming stood up and clasped her hands. 'I don't think anything, I don't know anything except this one thing — that you exist and that I'm dying of love for you.'

Inés allowed him to hold her hands and looked down at the floor with a thoughtful expression.

'You *have* heard something,' she said in a harsh rapid voice. 'Is it just about me or also about von Ribbing?'

'About you, they've said you are a dangerous coquette, nothing else.'

'And about von Ribbing?'

Flemming hesitated.

'Just say it. Something about adolescent girls?'

'Not only *that*,' said Flemming, blushing in embarrassment.

'What!' Inés looked at him in surprise. She pulled her hands away and walked around, agitated. Then she sat down, leaned back and said calmly, 'That may not be true at all.'

'How did you end up married to that man?' Flemming said after a pause.

'There, finally you're asking a question,' Inés exclaimed, animated. 'But I don't feel like telling you today.'

'Is he cruel to you?'

'No, I can't really say that. But insanely jealous, although I never meddle in his affairs, and in reality have almost never been his wife.'

'You're surprised that he stands for it,' Inés continued when Flemming seemed to want to say something but then gave up. 'Yes, it's rather astonishing, but at the time he was already so dissipated. What he wanted to force me to do was loathsome beyond words. He thought about getting a divorce but then his lawyer advised him not to do it for his own sake.'

'Then I think you must have the freedom to do what you want.'

'Ah yes, freedom. What does that mean? According to the law he can drag me into court and have me condemned the day he discovers something.' Inés again looked dark and brooding.

'If only we could fly to the ends of the earth and hide away from all people.'

'Yes, if only one could,' Inés mumbled absently.

'If I had money and there were no obstacles, would you, Inés?' Flemming asked in a low trembling voice.

'No. According to my beliefs, a marriage cannot be dissolved.'

'But when there isn't a marriage and people aren't faithful to each other,' Flemming was on the point of saying.

'Although the marriage would still be in force even if I left,' Inés continued, 'so that's not the reason. But how long would it last, do you suppose?'

'The love between us?' Flemming looked at her with a frightened expression.

'Remember, I'm so much older than you.'

'I can answer for myself,' Flemming said quietly. 'I would never, never stop loving you.'

'We have no idea about that,' Inés shook her head sadly. 'And also'—a faint blush rose in her cheeks—'I still don't know if you are the one who could...' She seemed to forget what she intended to say.

'Be enough for you?' Flemming's voice sounded as if it was breathed out in a large empty space.

'Yes, or,'—she took a deep breath—'I don't think I can love like other women can.'

'*You!*' Flemming got up and came over to her, but Inés suddenly sprang up, ran to the farthest corner of the room, leaned her forehead against the wall and sobbed.

Flemming followed, but stopped a step away from her. He didn't dare touch her.

In a little while Inés straightened up, dried her face, and turned toward him.

'I can't bear to see you unhappy, Inés,' whispered Flemming, with a painfully contracted face. 'I would rather disappear.'

Inés threw herself into his arms and pressed him to her. 'It's you I'm thinking about, Arthur. You are too good, too complete, and too innocent to lose yourself for my sake. Oh, such a treasure, and what do you get in return?'

'Don't talk like that, Inés. What am I in comparison to you?'

'You are everything and I am nothing,' Inés whispered with her mouth against his throat. 'Oh I'm so frightened, Arthur, now that I know you better and understand—I can cause your destruction.'

'Yes, if you let me go. You've become everything to me. If I lose you, I lose everything. Promise you won't leave me, Inés.'

'Oh Arthur, my own, my beloved. I feel at this moment that I could give my life for you.'

They held each other in a long embrace. Then Inés said, 'My eyes are burning, I have to go in and bathe them.'

'I'll come and watch.'

'If you like,' Inés walked ahead and he followed.

'Sit over there on the chaise longue. I'll be finished soon.' Inés bent over the marble washstand and with a sponge let the cold water trickle down her face.

Flemming's eyes roved around the room with an almost worshipful expression.

'So this is where you sleep,' he asked when Inés had straightened up and grabbed a hand towel.

'Yes, I lie there every night and can't fall asleep because I'm thinking of you,' Inés tilted her head toward the bed. 'And when I finally do get to sleep, that's when you really become a burden.'

Flemming sprang up.

'No, sit right there, ' she held out her hand with the towel in warning. 'It's enough to have you causing a ruckus at night. Shall I now have no peace from you while I make a small mid-day toilette?'

Flemming resumed his former place. 'When you smile at me and joke,' he said, 'a feeling flows through me—it's indescribable, I lose my senses,' he clutched his head with both hands.

'Well now everything should be fine for you,' Inés answered, 'because now I'm going to smile and joke the whole day.' She stood in front of the mirror and lightly went over her hair with a silver brush.

'Listen, Arthur,' she continued a minute later, turning abruptly toward him. 'We'll cut loose today, find something amusing and dangerous.'

'Yes!' Flemming shouted, and clapped his hands.

'But what? There are so many places where we absolutely can't risk being seen together—should we take a carriage and drive to Ejub and the Sweet Waters, and lie down in the grass under the sheltering trees…' She pondered a bit.

'No, to Stambul,' she said in a decisive tone. 'That's the safest place to avoid meeting anyone. Have you been to the Turkish restaurants over there—no? So we'll do it. They're part of the sights of Turkey. Hurry on ahead. I'll take the tram and you go on foot; then we can meet outside the station building down in Galata. We'll take a cab from there.'


'Oh, we have to give up talking to each other,' Inés said to Flemming, leaning back in the open cab under the large sunshade. They were driving at a snail's pace with constant stops through the throngs on the Galata bridge, and it took a powerful voice to be heard over the shouts and commotion

*Kara-Keui (Galata) bridge, Constantinople,*
Postcard 1890-1900

around them.

So they sat quietly. Flemming had pulled the glove off Inés's hand, which he held in his.

When they had crossed the bridge and were coming past the Sublime Porte up the hill to Hagia Sophia, where there was not so much traffic, the coachman began to whip the horse, and at a brisk trot they drove through Stambul's narrow streets.

'All right, this is as far as we go,' Inés said.

Flemming stood up, poked the coachman in the back with his stick, and immediately afterwards they climbed out.

'You can wait,' Inés told the driver in Greek, and took Flemming's arm.

They took a few steps along the narrow street, which lacked paving or sidewalks, where garbage lay in heaps on both sides next to the irregular Turkish houses with grated windows on the second floor, and where food being cooked outside filled the air with a spicy-sweet and sickly odor.

'We'll go in here,' Inés said, lifting her skirt as she stepped over a gutter awash with curdled milk and half-chewed bones in front of a house with a grey masonry façade, no windows and a tall, narrow gate.

Inés pushed open the gate, and before them lay a little stone stairway which they descended into a courtyard surrounded by high vine-covered walls, along which were small alcoves whose walls were made of lattice work and half-dead creepers, with tables and chairs for two or four.

In one of the corners by the house doorway a kitchen was set up, where an old Turk in a green turban was bending over a cooking pot. Squatting close to him was a second Turk who was washing dishes. An adolescent boy in blue Turkish trousers, gold turban, and red tunic with tucked up arms was wiping tables; and in a couple of alcoves there were Arabs silently eating and some Turks smoking their *narghile* with its long pipe emitting a heavy, sweetish smoke.

Inés took a place in one of the alcoves where the rectangular stone table was placed between two low cane chairs without backs.

'Can't we have a room for ourselves?' Flemming asked.

Inés laughed. 'Do you want to be up in the *harem*?'

Flemming looked around.

'Are you crazy!' Inés said quickly, tugging at his jacket. 'Remember they are Turks, and, more than that, the proprietor over there has a green turban. Do you think they would tolerate a male *giaour* casting his unclean eyes on their holy bordellos? Sit down for a minute or you'll be shot right away.'

Flemming sat down on the chair opposite her.

Inés called out a Turkish word and the young boy came over to them. He touched his hand to his head, then to his chest, and finally down to the ground.

'Bring us coffee and sorbet,' Inés said, 'and a plate of *pilaf*.'

'Did you notice how beautiful he was?' she asked when the boy was gone. 'Fine as a young stallion of the noblest breed.'

'I think Turks look so strangely sad,' Flemming observed.

'No, but serious and calm. It must be their religion that makes them passive and fatalistic. Whatever happens to them, happens to them, so they believe. And they have such dignity! Just look at our stallion of a waiter! Don't you think he has the gait and bearing of a *Grand Vizier*?'

The Turkish boy brought their order. He carried the tray on his head.

Flemming found the *pilaf* impossible to eat. Inés laughed at his pitiful expressions.

'When we've smoked our last cigarette, let's go,' Inés said.

'No, let's stay as long as possible,' Flemming begged. 'It's so amazingly wonderful sitting here. I can imagine that I've carried you away to a place far in the East and that nobody can come and take you away from me.'

'Now that is a delightful thought! And then this silence.'

'Whatever they do, these Turks, they do it so quietly, and then they never speak.'

'And the din from the street? It's like it's disappeared from the face of the earth.'

'Yes,' said Inés. 'The walls are so thick, and then the café is lower than the street. It's like we're sitting at the bottom of a well.'

A while later they got ready to leave. Inés paid. 'Twenty *piastres*, that's certainly cheap entertainment,' she said to Flemming as she was standing up.

'I believe you also left a gold coin on the tray,' said Flemming, as they came outside.

'That was *bachtsisch* for the *Grand Vizier*,' Inés answered cheerfully.

'No wonder he bowed to the earth three times for you.'

'He got it because he was so beautiful to look at and because I'm so happy today.'

'Where are we going now?' Flemming asked imploringly.

'I have to go home, remember, I have to eat and get dressed — the opera starts at eight o'clock.'

'You don't eat until seven.' Flemming nervously squeezed her fingers.

Inés shook her head.

'Smyrna Street, number 11,' she said to the driver, when they had seated themselves. 'I was just teasing you.' She leaned back in the cab and laughed.

'I am consumed by happiness, Inés.' Flemming pulled his hat lower down on his forehead.

'It's nearly five,' she said, as they drove across the Galata Bridge. 'Look at the *mullahs* in their long capes and white turbans, how they hurry to be on time for the call to prayer. In a little while you'll hear it sung from all the minaret balconies around here — Allah, Allah, von Dallah!' she sang merrily in the *mullahs'* mournful tones.

'Today you are not afraid,' Flemming said, enchanted, 'even though we're driving in an open cab.'

'Not a bit! If we met von Ribbing with the Minister and all the rest, you'd see me stand up in the cab and shout that we've been to visit the *Grand Vizier* and looked at a stallion that was for sale.'

'I think you've gone mad, Inés.'

'Yes, completely! If Averding came walking by with one of the juveniles on each arm, I'd invite him to come up and visit our bachelor rooms on Smyrna Street. Imagine if they knew what we're up to!' She burst into laughter.

'We'll drive over and say hello to Fru Ruder,' Flemming said gaily. 'I think we owe her that. Now I'll give the order,' he made a motion to stand up and call out to the driver.

At the end of the Galata Bridge with its sumptuous fruit stalls on both sides, the cab had to stop for a bit before it could advance. When they were again in motion, Inés pulled her parasol down over her face, and with a jerk pressed closer to Flemming.

'What *is* it?'

'Shhh, don't speak, don't move,' Inés whispered, gripping his arm. 'Sit absolutely still.'

Not until they had passed through Galata, which was bustling with Jews, and had begun to drive up the steep slope that led to the Pangalti Quarter, did Inés say, 'It was a man who walked past.'

'What kind of man?'

'A ragged old Greek who sells illegal medicines in the Phanar district. He makes his living by performing secret child-murder or whatever it's called. Just look, even today, in the midst of all our happiness — well, if something bad happens to me I won't be able to complain that I didn't have warnings.'

'It doesn't take more than that to frighten you,' Flemming exclaimed unhappily. 'I don't understand — lots of characters like that could have passed by us.'

'But this one here knows who I am, you must understand. Once a few years ago, he forced his way into the house under the pretense that he had something important to tell me. It was von Ribbing's secret that he wanted to sell. If I would come at a predetermined time I could hide and witness what was taking place. I showed him the door, naturally. But when he was leaving he said his name and his address, which I've remembered against my will.'

'He didn't see you, you can be sure of that.'

'No, I hope not — otherwise — he's probably von Ribbing's trusted henchman. I definitely think he looked at me, but he was terribly cross-eyed, I remember.'

'Well, thank heavens for that. Don't think about it any more,

Inés. We'll be there soon.' He slipped his arm around her waist.

'No, it was just for the moment that I felt so terribly afraid. We'll get out at the corner of the street and then you go in first. Draw the curtains in both rooms — I'm so hot and dusty. I can stay with you nearly an hour.'

# X

Sixteen days had gone by.

Inés was at a performance by the French Opera. She was sitting next to her husband in the front row of a crowded side box, wearing a salmon-red, low-cut silk dress, with flowers at her breast and in her hair. It was stiflingly hot and the air was heavy from the smell of powder and perfume and flowers.

It was the final performance and *Orpheus in the Underworld* was playing to a sold-out, jubilant house.

Inés wasn't following what was happening on the stage. Half-dead from the heat, her face hidden behind her large, white feather fan, the orchestra's exuberant playing of the familiar melodies swept past her ears.

The Ruders were sitting in the box across from them.

Inés was thinking about Flemming.

He wasn't there. Neither this evening nor yesterday evening had she seen him. For the twentieth time her eyes scanned the orchestra section where there were lots of tourists, the back of the hall under the balcony, all the boxes, the balcony, even the stage where they had set up extra chairs.

The previous evenings he had taken a seat at the end of the first row in the orchestra section and as soon as the curtain went up, she felt the gaze from his adoring eyes targeting her like magnetic charges every minute.

'Where was he now... what was he doing?' she asked herself with a nagging unease, while down on the stage fingers were pointed at Jupiter amid a chorus of laughter.

Poor, poor Arthur! He must have received her letter yesterday at lunchtime. While he was standing by the window waiting for her, it had arrived. He quickly ripped it open and read it; the letters danced before his eyes, and...

She felt a stab through her heart.

It must have struck him like lightening, though she had tried to prepare him the last times. But he hadn't wanted, hadn't dared to understand. Anxious and imploring, he had looked at her with his unbearably humble and searching gaze, and she was unable to get the words out of her mouth that she had come for the last time, but had left with the promise to see him the next day.

She had kept her promise one time, but broken it the next.

Instead she had written that it was over forever.

Poor, poor Arthur! But she *couldn't* do otherwise. She had to pull out of this terrible danger, before it was too late. Amazing that she hadn't been caught. All of their outings and rendezvous in Smyrna Street. And that Louis hadn't noticed her time after time sneaking out in the evening, not returning until right before von Ribbing came!

And during the dinner for the Swedish officers—any child must have been able to read the oblivious, insane infatuation in his eyes and on his face.

If he had been able to control himself or dissemble. Just a little. But he had been beside himself, looked at her as if they were alone, followed her, wanted to dance with her much too often, as at the ball on the corvette.

The Madonna should be eternally thanked because she had protected her. She would make a gift of money to St. Maria's hospital for the Sisters of Mercy right away.

And then settle back into her old routine. Gradually. For now she was in pain.

Since she had broken with him, she had felt a loss and an emptiness deep inside and the memories of their life together wrapped themselves around her mind like a sweet and painful melancholy, a melancholy that resembled longing and often brought tears to her eyes.

Not that she for one moment considered changing her resolve. Not even to free Arthur from the agony she knew he was suffering and the consequences it might have for him.

If only she had had the courage to tell him the truth. That would have pained him less.

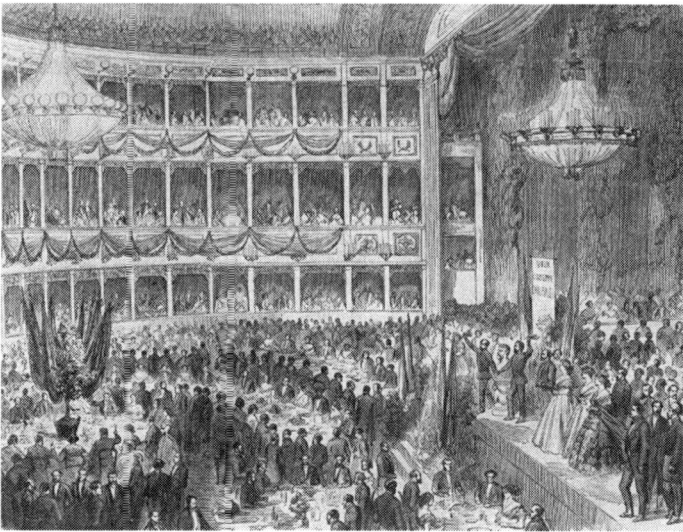

*The Naum theatre in Pera*

Built in 1848 on the site of an earlier wooden theatre that was destroyed by fire, this building served as the chief opera house of Constantinople, until ̄ too was destroyed by a fire in 1870.

What must he think of her now. Give herself to him as *she* had done and after a few weeks, throw him away like a toy. Her cheeks were burring with shame.

But she *could* and *would* not tell him the truth. This sad secret that nature had neglected her so cruelly — this she would take to the grave.

For now there was no longer any doubt.

Oh God, oh God! This insoluble riddle, this gap between desire and reality.

Her blood was restless and churning, her imagination filled with impure thoughts. When she lay in her bed at night, eyes closed, she felt Arthur in her arms, and tried to conjure forth an ecstasy she had never experienced from lovemaking.

She was tired and depressed. Her mind was disturbed and she was filled with self-loathing. When she performed her devotions in the chapel, she felt as if the Madonna turned away from her, and confession the other day had brought her no solace.

But of course she had not confessed everything to the holy father either.

Suddenly Inés saw the door open in the opposite box where the Ruders were sitting, and Averding appeared in the doorway. With a rapid movement he bent forward and holding onto the railing that separated the box from the one next to it, he slipped his other arm behind the gentlemen in the back row and grabbed Ruder's shoulder. Ruder quickly turned around and immediately left the box with Averding. At that moment the curtain fell and the audience clapped and shouted exultantly. Inés stood up, her face deathly pale, raised her seat and mumbling *pardon* rushed from the box and ran down the corridor, through the foyer and to the corridor on the opposite side of the house. Ruder and Averding were standing by a counter impatiently demanding their coats.

'Nonetheless she is the one who's behind it,' Inés heard Ruder say. 'Is there no one in the cloakroom, dammit!' He banged the counter with his cane. 'My wife has seen them together on the street, and I've seen quite enough myself here in the theater!'

'Where the hell are you going!' Von Ribbing's voice was right behind Inés, who had stopped a couple of steps away from the counter.

Just then Ruder had gotten his coat and turned around.

'Flemming has taken poison,' he said hurriedly to von Ribbing and rushed down the steps with Averding.

'Wait a minute! My hat, wait! Where does he live?!'

'Smyrna Street 11!' And a door slammed shut.

'I'll take a cab.' Von Ribbing left the corridor as quickly as his stiff legs allowed, taking no notice of Inés who stood like a statue, eyes staring.

She was suddenly aware that someone had pushed her and said *'Pardon, Madame,'* and then she noticed the crowd around her and that all the box doors were wide open.

Mechanically she pulled herself together, started to move her legs, reached the stairs which she descended, holding tightly onto the railing.

*'Bon soir, Madame! How are you, Ma'am!'* Several times she heard these words spoken by distant, hollow voices without understanding what they meant or knowing where they came from.

She'd come to the bottom of the stairs and forced her way through a crowd of people, through corridors and hallways with doors that shut behind her. Then she felt a breeze on her face, something was shouted, a whip was cracked, a carriage door snapped open, she was sitting on a seat cushion, was asked where she lived, named the place and was startled by the sound of her own voice.

When the cab started to move, Inés was thrown back in the corner of the carriage and she lay there without moving a limb until she got out on the Grande Rue de Pera.

The coachman opened the wrought iron gate, she stepped inside and moved with irregular steps down the garden's gravel path, entered the illuminated entry hall where she met a servant, noticed that he followed her up the staircase, thought she heard him say something, but didn't think to answer.

Then a glaring light blinded her eyes and after that she

walked through semi-darkness.

'I beg your pardon, Madame, but Louis is sick. Shall the lamps stay lit until the Master comes?'

'Do as you wish,' Inés said and discovered she was standing with her hand on the doorknob to her bedroom.

'Beg pardon, Madame, but has Madame been robbed?'

Inés looked down at her bare arms and shook her head.

'Beg pardon, Madame, but there is a letter for Madame in the balcony room. I will get it for Madame now.' He disappeared and came right back with a large envelope on a crystal tray.

Inés, who, like a sleepwalker, hadn't moved, took the letter and drifted into her bedroom.

She laid the letter on her dressing table where the candelabra was lit. Then she turned away with a shudder, took a couple of turns across the room, her eyes moving nervously and her lips pressed tightly together. Finally she sat down on the chair in front of the dressing table, picked up the letter and tore open the envelope. It contained, in addition to two small pages of writing, a packet of letters bound together with a ribbon.

Inés read:

Dear Inés,

You no longer love me, otherwise you wouldn't so cruelly and calmly have dropped me. How can that be, and what have I done to you?

It would have been better if you had told me that you no longer cared for me. Then I would at least have had the consolation that you found me worthy of your honesty. Because what you say is just a pretext.

Oh Inés, Inés, if you had loved me as I love you, what thoughts would you have had of danger, and why did you write these words: 'It is my firm, irrevocable decision and I implore you, both for your sake and for mine, not to attempt to change it.' Oh Inés, I would have understood that you were serious without these cold words that pierce my heart like a dagger.

You want your former calm and carefree life back, you say. You can't bear the constant tension in your life… Well, Inés, it shall be as you wish. I am prepared to disappear from your life, so that you will be content and happy as before.

When I got your letter yesterday it was as if my soul had been crushed to dust and I thought immediately: You must die, you *can't* do otherwise. But then it occurred to me how hard that would be on you, Inés, and I decided that I would live for your sake — you to whom I am indebted for an expanse of joy so large that the bitterest anguish of an entire life could not offset it. I felt as strong as a martyr willing to sacrifice himself for his faith. And I went to the office and sat down at my desk and opened the ledger and started to add up the numbers. But everything was swimming in front of my eyes and I did nothing until Ruder came and said I had a fever and let me go home.

But here in this room, Inés, here where you have been — the longing for death came over me once again and all night I have struggled to overcome it.

This morning I went to the office again and was again sent home and Ruder said he would send a doctor, but I asked him to wait until tomorrow.

I saw you on the street today, Inés. You got out of your carriage and went into a shop, and I grabbed onto a lamppost so I wouldn't sink to the ground. You looked so beautiful and radiant and then I thought about how you had put your arms around my neck and kissed my lips and that I had embraced you and possessed you completely, and now that would never happen again.

At that moment I made the decision to die and I felt an intense joy knowing there was a bottle of opium in the little medicine box my father had given me for the journey. It was as if a burden had fallen from me and my soul felt light and free. Soon the unbearable pain I was suffering would be over. I went to the Café Paris, ate something and drank half a bottle of wine. And then I read the newspapers. It felt so solemn to read the newspapers for the last time.

Averding came into the restaurant. He wanted me to go out with him tonight and I agreed to meet him at the café at 10:30. We chatted together for a while and he didn't notice anything different about me.

Afterwards I went home and read your letters, Inés, and pressed my lips against every word in them. Now you shall have them back. I thought about burning them, but I *couldn't*. I have written a letter to Ruder in which I said I had gambled and lost a large sum of money for which I received a reprieve until tomorrow, but that I would rather die, since I couldn't pay. So that no one should suspect or think anything about you, Inés.

When this letter has been put in an envelope, I will take it out to the postbox. Then you will get it tonight when you return from the opera. By that time I will already have been dead for five hours. I will lie down on the divan — *our* divan — Inés, my love — then I will empty the bottle, and then death comes.

I am not in despair, Inés. You see how calmly my hand is writing and how clear my thoughts are. If I were to live instead of die — I shudder at the thought.

And now, Inés, now I kneel before you in my thoughts, kiss your hands and look at you with a final, heartfelt prayer in my eyes: do not believe you are to blame for my death. It isn't you, Inés, it is fate. You know I have always been weary of life, before I saw you, Inés. I often thought about dying back then.

Do you remember when we walked in the cemetery and talked about dying and I thought death would be simple and sweet when you were with me.

And I have you with me, Inés, locked up inside my soul, in my last flash of consciousness, in my very last breath. And I know that you will also die soon. 'Even if I were to live to be a hundred years old, that's still not very far off,' you said in the cemetery. I hear those words inside me like the twittering of birds, Inés.

Now, when I shall write the last, terrible word, my hand shakes and my heart tightens. I must wait a little.

*Farewell,* Inés. There, now it's said. Thank you for the love you gave me. Thank you for all eternity.

*Your Arthur*

Inés's hands fell into her lap. Grief lay like a band of fire lashed tightly around her waist, and she rocked gently back and forth in the chair.

Suddenly she saw in the mirror a pale yellow face with sunken eyes, lines between her eyebrows and dead, black hair plastered to her forehead.

With a half-choked cry she slid down from the chair and lay on the floor supported by her knees and elbows, her face buried in her hands.

After a while she heard her husband in the next room. She got up quickly, blew out the candles, and in the next instant had crawled into bed and pulled the covers up to her chin.

The door opened and faint red light floated into the room.

'Are you sleeping, Inés?'

She gathered her strength and said out loud, 'No.'

'There was nothing to be done. Dead as a doornail.'

There was a pause, then Inés said, her teeth chattering, 'Was there no doctor?'

'The landlady had fetched one, but it was too late. We'll have to bury him over at Skutari—hmmm, who would have thought … '

'Had he suffered much?' Inés forced the words out with difficulty.

'Yes, well, who can know. He looked ugly. Ah yes, this will be a lovely report to make to his parents, thank you very much.'

'A strange boy,' he went on. 'And tactless! Addressing his final words to Ruder instead of me, how do you like that! Never heard anything like it. Taking your life in a city like Constantinople when you come from a hole like Sweden. And for the sake of a wretched gambling debt. He could have written to his father, or we could have helped him. The idiot.'

Von Ribbing waited a minute and then said gruffly: 'Damned if I don't think the fellow was crazy.' He turned on his heel and left the room.

Inés lay still until his footsteps died away. Then she broke into piercing sobs.

# XI

The von Ribbings were in Therapia. They had been staying there for ten weeks and it was now the beginning of October.

Their country home lay hidden in a dense garden on a scrubby slope that jutted out into the Bosporus.

A flat glass roof held up by slender vine-covered iron columns extended from under the second floor windows, covering the terrace in the front of the house.

On the bench in the corner of the terrace, Inés had spent most hours of the day enveloped in a silk morning gown, her slender hands, which had grown drawn and lifeless, resting on her lap, her feet in slippers.

Sometimes she sat in the summerhouse at the far end of the garden where she could hear the gentle waves of the Bosporus lapping. Then she closed her eyes and dreamt she was in the graveyard at Skutari where Arthur was buried, and where she too would be laid to rest one day.

Or she dreamt that he wasn't dead, but that she was sitting waiting for him. Then he came and his eyes shone with love and she took him in her arms and pressed his head to her breast and said she would never let him go.

In the beginning she had often thought she would take the boat over to Skutari, kneel by his grave, lay her face on the green grass and wet it with her tears. But every time she was about to do it, she collapsed in tears, so full of pain and anguish she thought her chest would explode.

And she felt sick and weak as well. It felt as if the strength in her body had faded and disappeared. It was an effort to drag herself around the house and garden. When she sat down she would often doze off and her anxious brooding was replaced by oppressive reverie.

When von Ribbing didn't bring home guests from the city, he most often ate dinner alone. As soon as he was expected, Inés went up to her rooms and had the servant say that she wasn't feeling well. Her head ached and she felt nauseated all the time.

'You have jaundice,' von Ribbing said when he saw her. And occasionally he added, 'Very odd that you don't send for a doctor. But I suppose it's a novelty to walk around like a ghost for a while.'

His tone was malicious, almost happy. It gave him satisfaction to see her faded and broken down, this woman whose healthy youth and vigorous beauty had irritated him for so long. He enjoyed going to dinners and parties given by Therapia's prominent summer residents without her, for when she was by his side he was always reduced to insignificance.

It was an afternoon in the first week of October. Inés had ordered the coachman to hitch the horses. She came down the stairs to the courtyard wearing her long black cashmere cloak, her face covered with a veil.

The groom opened the carriage door.

'To Phanar,' Inés said and climbed in.

They drove through Therapia past the villas and magnificent palaces of the foreign ambassadors, out onto the elegant promenade along the Bosporus.

The road which at certain times of the day was bustling with carriages and equestrians of both sexes was now practically empty, and Inés could abandon herself to her thoughts without the disruption of greetings. She leaned back in the carriage, her eyes half closed, and felt the heavy beating of her heart as a physical pain.

It had taken her a long time to decide to take this step. Day after day went by and the decision she had made in the morning had not been carried out by the time evening came.

Finally one day she was on her way. On her way to crime and disgrace in order to save herself from death. Because there was no choice: either she must obliterate the consequences of her affair with Arthur or voluntarily seek death.

Over there on the other side of the Bosporus lay Skutari. If

*Phanar,* Postacard, undated (ca.1900)

she lifted her eyes, she would be able to glimpse the cemetery in the distance. But she couldn't bear to nor did she dare. Not now when she would be returning with the criminal substance that would destroy the future life she carried under her heart. It would be many long years, when she had been chastened and cleansed through penance and deeds of charity, before she would dare turn her face toward that holy place where he was buried, he whose young life had been taken so abruptly because of her heedlessness.

Oh, if only she had his courage. This pure and perfect soul who gladly took leave of a life whose burden he could not bear.

But she did not dare to enter the dreadful torments of purgatory with so much guilt and sin not atoned for. She would have to live to make herself worthy of the Madonna's mercy. When she had gotten through this, she would renounce the world, enter St. Maria's blessed hospital and become a Sister of Mercy for the rest of her life. This she had sworn with her lips on the crucifix.

Then the Mother of God, through her intercession, would make sure her punishment was short and easy.

If only her strength didn't fail her. Wouldn't she be paralyzed by shame and agony when she stepped into his shop and made herself an accomplice and confidante of this scoundrel of a Greek?

So deep had she sunk. She would stand before von Ribbing's criminal henchman as a humble client. She moaned softly and wet her burning lips with her tongue.

And could she be sure of his silence, even if she paid for it dearly? Nervously her hand searched in her pocket to feel that the money was there.

They drove by the imperial palace, Çiragan, the Sultan's summer residence, its gold and marble glittering in the sun, and Dolmabahçe, the winter palace with its shady park and gleaming white walls, while Inés's disquiet grew greater and greater—they would soon be there.

At the entrance to Phanar she signalled the coachman that he should stop.

'Wait here until I return,' she said after she had stepped out and mumbled something about Greek jewelry.

Oh God, oh God, this was worse than death. Oh God, what a wretched person she had become.

She walked down a long and dismal street lined with little stalls and shops and low buildings that resembled dismantled fortresses. Her feet were ankle deep in dust and filth which in the long drought had decomposed to a powder, and she did not lift up the train of her dress.

At the entrances to the shops sat the Greek shopkeepers smoking their pipes with lazy eyes, as if they had given up on looking for customers.

Here and there tattered children lay next to the stinking gutter propelling paper *caiques* with their hands and wooden sticks.

Not a sound could be heard in the long, deserted street. A few veiled women with blue and cherry-red *feredscher* went from shop to shop without haggling or looking at the wares displayed on the tables that stuck out onto the street.

Inés slunk forward, her knees shaking, her breathing shallow. The astonished looks of those she passed pierced her like needles, even though her eyes were downcast so she would not have to see them.

From time to time she stood still and pressed her hands to her heart. Was it she who had set out on this journey, was bound for this place, she, the beautiful, celebrated Inés? She felt her throat choke up and stinging tears forced their way out.

And was it possible that it was only three months ago she had taken the steamer from Prinkipo, and sat in the stern of the boat so proud and happy and self-assured?

Alas, if only she and Arthur had been struck dead on the way to Pera when the cable broke. How immeasurably better that would have been for them both.

Oh, such a fate. No one in the world could possibly ever have suffered as much as she had during these months. 'Madonna, Madonna! Have mercy on me.' She let the rosary hanging on her belt glide through her trembling fingers while her pale grey lips recited prayers in a mumble.

'It isn't you, it's fate,' Arthur had written. Yes, it had to be fate that had made her blind, with no thought to what could happen to her.

No, not without a thought. At the time it had sometimes flashed through her head as a possibility, but not in a way that made her frightened.

If only she survived this, she would give thanks for her suffering. The suffering would make her more worthy of him, who out of love for her had sought death.

She lifted her eyes and looked through her veil at the number on the nearby building. A few more steps and she would be at his place. She saw him standing in the middle of the entryway to his shop, his hands deep in the pockets of his *fustanelle*.

'Hurry up, hurry up,' she said to herself. 'In ten minutes it will be over and you will be saved.'

But no, she *couldn't*. It was as if her feet had taken root. Not today, another time — she turned and walked back.

'Another time, another time,' she kept saying to herself. 'There's no rush either.'

Would she have the courage another time? she thought a moment later, and a hopeless weariness crept over her. Wouldn't it go like today? Her ears were ringing, and it was as if her chest caved in.

*Was* there no other way out? *Must* she go to this man? Wouldn't it be better to confide in a doctor? Or — a flash of relief shot through her — she had suddenly remembered the midwife at the corner of Smyrna Street whose sign she had seen the first time she left Arthur's place.

It would be a thousand times better to go to her. She would never find out what her name was or her position, and in any case she was a woman like herself.

'Oh heavenly Madonna, I thank you,' she whispered, and big tears of relief rolled down her cheeks. Now she was certain the Madonna had compassion for her. In a week's time they would move to Constantinople and then she would sneak over there in the evening darkness.

Suddenly she heard a rapid, hoarse and anguished wheezing. It sounded as if it came from a sack that had been cinched tight or from something buried alive.

Inés shuddered and turned around.

Twenty steps away a huge cloud of dust was hurtling toward her, stirred up by a pack of racing dogs who were biting and tearing at something oblong and pink that ran and fell down, ran and fell down.

As the pack got closer, Inés discovered that the muffled, otherworldly whine was coming from the pink object in front, and in the next instant, that the pink thing was also a dog, skinned alive from snout to tail, eyes bulging, tongue hanging down to the ground, dragging its coat, steaming and turned inside out, behind it through the dried-out filth in the street.

Inés recoiled to the side, supporting herself with her back against the wall of a building. 'Is there no one who takes pity,' her lips mumbled the soundless words as her helpless gaze slid across the row of houses in the long street, where the children continued their play undisturbed and the shop-keepers remained calmly seated, faces expressionless as their eyes followed the charging spectacle.

It was very close to Inés now. The victim fell down and rolled over while the pursuers bit and tore, then got up, ran and fell again, incessantly emitting this hoarse, helpless sound. Dust and filth stuck to the animal's bloody body and formed clumps in the gaping wounds.

Then a white-bearded old man in a worn *fustanelle* and leather-rimmed cap stepped out of a shop across from Inés and pressed a brass *mangan* lid, welded to the end of a long pipe, down on the savaged animal body, covering it. The animal collapsed with a weak, rattling whimper. The pursuing dogs sniffed around the lid to make sure their victim was dead and then did an about-face, and barking, charged back in the direction they'd come.

For Inés it was as if she had seen in a single glimpse the sum of the world's anguish and horror and pain. Fear of death had shot through her like an ice-cold beam. And when she stood upright in order to walk on, she sank helplessly to the ground.

*Group of dogs in the Grande Rue de Pera*
Postcard, undated (ca. 1900)

Veiled women came out with a chair and water in an earthenware bowl. They lifted Inés up, sat her in the chair, moved her veil to the side and sprinkled water on her face.

After a while she opened her eyes and tried to stand up, but wasn't able to.

One of the women went into the house and came back with naphtha in a cup which she held to Inés's lips.

Inés drank it, sat a little longer, tried again to stand up and was able to support herself. With a mute, thankful greeting to the women, who bowed, she walked down the street and came to her carriage, which she climbed into with great effort.

Inés cried silently. A vague notion of life's inexorable laws dawned on her and for the first time in her life, she thought about her husband with charity and compassion.

Were the Turks perhaps right with their fatalistic belief that whatever was meant to be, would happen? No, they were not right.

The dog, for example. If it had been satisfied with what it had and stayed in its own street, it wouldn't have been attacked and so miserably killed. That's how it was with her too. Oh, why hadn't she been satisfied with what she had?

Suddenly she sat up and stared wildly ahead. The dream she'd had on Prinkipo came to her like a vision, of the bloody, howling dog dragging itself through the dust and desiccated filth. The ice-cold terror from before shot through her again. Now she knew. She was the dog and she would die like it had.

At the same moment she was overcome by violent cramping in her belly. She pressed herself against the back of the carriage and bit into her handkerchief to stop the screams forcing themselves out through her cold lips.

When they arrived home and the groom opened the carriage door, she couldn't get up and the blue silk damask seat was stained with blood. The servant carried her upstairs and put her to bed.

While Inés had been gone a telegram had arrived, announcing that von Ribbing was staying in Constantinople for a few days and that Louis should come to the house in Pera. Louis had left immediately.

Almost a week passed before von Ribbing appeared at the country house.

When he got out of the carriage, he saw a one-horse buggy in the courtyard and as he stepped into the entrance hall, a stooped gentleman with a grey beard and wearing a light grey English suit was descending the stairs from the second floor.

'How do you do, Doctor,' von Ribbing said, extending his hand in greeting. 'It pleases me that Mrs. Ribbing has finally sent for you. She has been ailing since we came out here.'

'It would have pleased me more, and presumably you as well, had it happened earlier,' the doctor answered gravely.

'Is it something serious?' von Ribbing asked, his eyes attentive.

'Mrs. Ribbing will be dead before morning,' was the answer.

'What's that!' Von Ribbing staggered backwards.

'Had I been called right away instead of yesterday, I could possibly have saved her. Now there is nothing to be done.' The doctor put on his hat and started to leave.

Von Ribbing held him back. 'But in God's name, what is she dying from?' he asked in desperation.

'From…' The doctor stopped and then said, 'From a hemorrhage.'

'Good heavens! Who would have thought — as healthy and vigorous as she was. It just goes to show — it's a good thing we don't have children, because that kind of tendency is hereditary.'

The doctor shrugged his shoulders, said goodbye and left.

Von Ribbing tiptoed up the stairs and listened at the door of Inés's bedroom. He heard a muffled sound as from someone speaking continuously, far away.

The black servant Jean, who was the chambermaid, came up with an ice pack in a basin.

'What is this?' von Ribbing said. 'Why haven't you let me know what was going on?'

'Madame forbade it. Madame begged and pleaded the whole time that I shouldn't let anyone know that Madame was sick. Madame wouldn't hear of calling a doctor.'

'Hmm,' von Ribbing stared straight ahead with a vacant expression.

'It wasn't until Madame lost consciousness that I dared to do it on my own,' Jean went on. 'Madame has suffered so terribly. Then the doctor came and yesterday evening the doctor sent a nurse.'

'Is she here now?'

'Yes, she's sitting at the bedside reciting prayers.'

Von Ribbing opened the door and stepped in. There lay Inés stretched out in the bed under a sheet that covered her like a shroud. Her red swollen face was unrecognizable, and she was talking out loud, out of breath and without interruption.

Von Ribbing stood horrified. Then he gestured to the nurse and she and Jean left the room.

Von Ribbing walked over to the bed, bent down over Inés and took her hand.

'Do you recognize me, Inés?'

Inés went on speaking incoherently.

'Forgive me, Inés, for taking you as my wife!' he burst out, in a wail.

Inés turned her eyes and looked at him for a second. 'Yes, yes,' she whispered thickly. 'Now the old man is bringing the *mangan* lid.'

That night she died.

# Glossary

Skram included a number of foreign words and phrases in her novel which we have left untranslated, for the most part. We have retained her spelling; alternative spellings are indicated below in parentheses.

*bachtsisch (baksheesh)*
a tip or small bribe offered for past or future services

*caique (kayik)*
long, narrow rowboat used on the Bosporus

*feredscher (ferajeh, feraæce)*
cloak worn by Muslim women outside the home

*fustanelle (fustanella)*
traditional skirt-like garment worn by men in the Balkans

*giaour (gavur)*
word used by the Turks to describe all who are not Muslims, with especial reference to Christians; unbeliever

*Grand Vizier*
chief officer or minister of state in the Ottoman Empire.

*green turban*
Turks wearing green turbans were descendants of the Prophet, Mohammed

*guarda!*
 a warning cry called out to avert collision

*karnap*
a bay or enclosed room that projects from the façade of a building and is supported by pillars or brackets

*kava'er (kavass)*
 a consular guard in the countries of the Levant

*mangan*
a metal pan for holding burning charcoal or coals

*narghile (nargile)*
waterpipe; hookah

*stambuline*
long-tailed frock coat worn by Turkish officials in the 19th century

# Translators' Note

In *Fru Inés* Amalie Skram created a living image of Constantinople in the late nineteenth century. The administrative capital of the Ottoman Empire, Constantinople was a city in the throes of change. Increasing trade with European powers had led to an influx of foreigners pursuing their varied commercial and diplomatic interests. The ancient city was increasingly a cosmopolitan mixture of east and west, populated by foreign businessmen, diplomats and travellers. As translators our task was to do for our readers what Skram did for hers: to render faithfully the things she described many years after her visits to the city and its environs in the early 1870s. Skram wrote *Fru Inés* in 1891 when she was living in Copenhagen. In a letter to her publisher Paul Langhoff, she told him:

> I'm working harder on this novel than I have *ever* done before. It's because the story takes place in Constantinople and because I must dig and dig in my brain in order to bring the city alive in my mind's eye, the city, the people, the life, atmosphere etc. It's not because it's been 12 years since I last was there, but because everything there is so varied and complex, so rich and full of color.

Two years earlier while working on her big Bergen novel, *S.G. Myre*, she offered a similar description of her method of composition in a letter to her husband Erik Skram:

> I have to be occupied for a long time with my memory, imagination, fragments of information or knowledge about the things I'm dealing with, be occupied for a long time

until everything I want to portray—people [both inside and out], interiors, street scenes, and everything you can think of—the smells, the atmosphere, etc.—until I have *all of it*—every single bit of it photographically in my mind and moreover *know* everything these people think, feel and say, wish for or may do. That is my actual, true work when I'm writing. (And repeating it on paper once I have it inside is far easier.)

Skram writes about the laborious effort of drawing into her consciousness a thin strand of memories, tightly coiled and elastic. Sometimes the strand slips and springs back before she has drawn it out completely, and then she must again start to dig and search. In the case of *Fru Inés* the memories would have been from voyages with her husband, ship's captain August Müller, to the Black Sea, during which she made several visits to Constantinople and its environs. Stambul, the old Turkish city, occupied the peninsula bounded by the Sea of Marmara, the Bosporus, and its inlet the Golden Horn. Across the Golden Horn was Galata, founded by Genoese traders in the thirteenth century and afterwards mostly inhabited by the Greek, Armenian and Jewish populace. On the heights above the crowded streets of Galata was Pera, the European quarter, where foreign embassies, business houses, and wealthy residences were located. Across the Bosporus on the Asian side was Skutari. As the beautiful young wife of Captain Müller, Skram would most likely have spent most of her time with the Europeans in Pera. But the novel reveals familiarity with the sights and sounds of many regions of the city and its waterways.

In *Fru Inés* it is perhaps not too fanciful to suggest that the strand Skram pulls out of her memory is one end of a reel of film. On this film strip is what her camera eye recorded: the people and motions of a great city in flux. While many of Skram's novels include vivid descriptions of a wide variety of cityscapes and settings, in *Fru Inés* her descriptions are cinematic as well as pictorial. Her characters are constantly on the move—walking the sea paths of the hotel on Prinkipo

Island, sailing through the Sea of Marmara into the Golden Horn, exploring the streets and parks and cemeteries of the Constantinople suburbs of Galata and Pera, riding in an open carriage across the crowded Galata Bridge and through the crooked streets of Stambul, and finally, wading through dust and filth on a street in the suburb of Phanar.

As the wife of a wealthy Swedish banker and consul, Fru Inés enjoys the luxurious life of the city's European businessmen and dignitaries. She resides in Pera during the winter months, spends summers in the wealthy Bosporus village of Therapia, and travels to the Princes' Islands in the Sea of Marmara to take sea baths at a spa hotel. Fru Inés is not a European, however, but a Spanish Levantine. Only brief mention is made of her home—Alexandria, one of three great port cities of the Levant—and her former circumstances: von Ribbing claims to have rescued her from her father's financial ruin.

As a denizen of the Levant—those lands on the shores of the eastern Mediterranean which were part of the Ottoman Empire from the sixteenth century to the twentieth— Inés is conversant in several languages, including French, Italian, Spanish, English, Greek, Turkish and Swedish. By the nineteenth century, *lingua franca*, a language made up of simplified Arabic syntax and mostly Italian and Spanish vocabulary and used by Mediterranean sailors and traders since the Middle Ages, had been replaced by French as the language of communication between east and west. But French was only one among many languages heard in the ports and on city streets, an experience that must have fascinated Amalie Skram, who grew up in the port city of Bergen where the docks were the center of city life. There she would have heard English, an assortment of European languages, and countless dialects from up and down the Norwegian coast.

The novel's cosmopolitan array of characters address Inés in their native languages and she responds sometimes in their language, sometimes in French. In the street she addresses men in Greek and Turkish. In our translation we have retained the original dialogue specified by Skram. Likewise we have kept the Turkish words, in Skram's spelling, which describe the sounds and sights in the city, all those objects and articles of clothing that make the city seem so foreign and exotic. These words appear in italics in the text and are explained in a glossary.

We have also included maps and pictures from the period so readers might visualize characters' movements and scenes from the novel: Inés and Flemming climbing the steps from Galata to Pera after the accident on the funicular; the packs of dogs who claim their territory on every city street; the opera house where Averding's sudden appearance in the box opposite Inés pierces her with dread just as the curtain falls on Jacques Offenbach's irreverent parody *Orpheus in the Underworld*. As translators we have endeavored to identify and correctly name buildings, streets and neighborhoods. Placenames in Turkey are no longer the same as when Skram visited the region; we have consulted maps and travel journals from the late nineteenth century as well as more recent books on the area and its history.

In his book *Levant. Splendour and Catastrophe on the Mediterranean*, historian Philip Mansel defines the Levant—a word originating from the French levant and meaning rising, where the sun is rising—as a Western name for an Eastern area and therefore, by implication, a dialogue between East and West. Skram's character Fru Inés exemplifies such a dialogue. She is a Spanish Levantine from Alexandria; a Roman Catholic in a city where most Christians are Greek Orthodox; and in a move that would advance her socially and economically, became the wife of a Swedish consul. In her search for fulfillment and freedom, she moves between different worlds in Constantinople, as was the norm among the different ethnic, religious and national groups living there. She makes clear in the first chapter her wish to maintain a certain fluidity when she rejects the title of "Consulinde" in favor of her unique identity "Fru Inés".

With her young Swedish lover, Inés recklessly ventures into worlds off limits to women of her station. Flemming takes lodgings at the end of a dead-end street called Smyrna, a safe haven where he and Inés can have their trysts, a place the lovers merrily refer to as their den of iniquity. Old maps indicate that there was indeed a small street called Smyrna near the Pancaldi quarter, but during the years Skram visited the region the name Smyrna was legendary—an important Mediterranean port city, busier even than Constantinople and referred to by travellers as "the pearl of the Levant". Known for its excellent wines, its taverns and cafés, Smyrna was a city of pleasure and sexual freedom. For a few hectic days, perhaps weeks, the rooms on Smyrna Street were an escape, a place where Inés and Flemming were free to give themselves over to pleasure. As Flemming once remarked to Inés, her mood was never darkened by superstition or fear while the couple were together on Smyrna Street.

But the apartment could provide only the illusion of freedom. Reality in the form of a pregnancy would open the door to the world's censure. In Inés's desperate carriage ride to seek the help of an abortionist, Skram's camera eye records her movement through different strata of society. Glittering mansions and palaces and the elegant promenade along the Bosporus give way to impoverished streets of collapsing wooden houses. In Skram's unsparing portrayal, the city with its hidden neighborhoods and quiet graveyards is also a city of mosques and churches, a place of harsh judgements and cruel consequences.

Katherine Hanson and Judith Messick

# Amalie Skram's Novel
## *Fru Inés*

Most of Amalie Skram's novels are set in Norway, either in the capital Kristiania or in the west country, in Bergen and the surrounding area. When it became known that she had chosen Constantinople as the setting for her third 'novel of marriage', the reaction was one of scepticism, bordering on lack of interest. The few reviewers who wrote about the novel wondered whether she was embarking on a new direction in her writing, moving away from the naturalistic style which had been her distinguishing feature. Had she too been gripped by the growing fascination with the Orient, in the same way as had Baudelaire, for example? Parts of *The Arabian Nights* had been translated into French at the beginning of the eighteenth century. And the Italian Edmondo de Amicis' travelogue *Constantinople* from 1876, which had been translated into Danish in 1888 from the fourteenth edition of the original, as it says on the title page, must have been well known. Edvard Brandes, who reviewed *Fru Inés* in the Danish newspaper *Politiken*, was of the opinion that Amalie Skram's descriptions of the city were more vibrant than de Amicis'. Nonetheless it seems that few – if any – readers seriously considered that this naturalist writer might have had a specific intention when she set the story of this novel's beautiful but unhappy protagonist in precisely this city. Why did she do that? Did the city add some new element to this story of love and marriage? It is clearly more than just a backdrop or a stage set; it is a vital part of the drama.

To understand the significance of this, we need to look back at her development as an author. Who was Amalie Skram when in 1891 she published *Fru Inés* with a small Copenhagen publisher, together with other stories which had previously been published in various journals, and gave the whole collection the title of *Love in North and South*?

She was born in Bergen in 1846. When she was not quite eighteen her father went bankrupt and emigrated to America. Soon after that, she married ship's captain Bernt August Müller and travelled with him in his sailing ship on her first long voyage from London to the West Indies. In 1871 she travelled with him again, this time on a world tour; they took with them their two small sons. They also took a complete library, and she learnt English and French, according to Liv Køltzow, who wrote a biography of Amalie Skram's early years. They called at Melbourne in Australia, Lima in Peru, and Constantinople. Later Amalie was to visit the city again, possibly more than once. But for the time being she kept her impressions to herself.

In 1877 she had a serious breakdown in connection with escalating marital conflict, which ended in separation and finally divorce. Just before that she had published her first literary review, and from then until her debut as a novelist in 1885 she wrote almost thirty reviews and articles. She wrote about the leading authors of the time, both Scandinavian and foreign; she was also enthusiastic about them in her letters, especially those to the Danish writer Erik Skram, who became her second husband in 1884. And she read the Bible. She collected impressions from real life, from what she observed and experienced, and she collected them from her reading. And of course she used her imagination.

Frederik Hegel, head of the leading Danish publisher Gyldendal, considered Amalie Skram's first novel *Constance Ring* too scandalous to be published under his imprint; she had to publish it herself on commission with a small publishing house in Kristiania. But there is no doubt that she was from the first regarded as one of the most courageous and high-profile authors in Norway and Denmark. Her next novel of marriage was *Lucie* (1888), whose sexually experienced protagonist is the mistress of a lawyer, Theodor Gerner. He becomes so besotted by her that he marries her, only to find that his project to turn her into a respectable bourgeois wife is doomed to failure. This novel can be seen as a counterpoint to Skram's two novels about inexperienced young girls who are married to experienced men, *Constance Ring* and the later *Forrådt* (*Betrayed*, 1892) which was published a year after *Fru Inés*. Between the novels of marriage Skram also began work on her major tetralogy *Hellemyrsfolket* (*The People of Hellemyr*), of which the first two volumes were published in 1887 and the final volume not until 1898. And in 1895 she published two novels about mental breakdown, *Professor Hieronimus* and *På St. Jørgen* (published jointly in English as *Under Observation*). These novels were based on her own experiences of treatment in mental institutions in Copenhagen and Roskilde, and sparked a vociferous debate about treatment of the mentally ill in Denmark.

In Amalie Skram's first novel there is a debate between the young wife Constance and her more experienced married friend about the institution of marriage. Constance complains about what she calls 'compulsory marital duties'; she calls marriage a 'dreadful institution' and goes so far as to say that it is a kind of legal prostitution. It was sentences like this which the editors of the journal *Nyt Tidsskrift* wished to delete when she submitted a few chapters to them. And it is likely that it was these sentiments about marriage which led Hegel to reject the novel when he read it in proof.

*Fru Inés* contains no explicit criticism of the institution of marriage. Nevertheless, it can be read as a continuation of the criticism expressed by Constance. In the centre of this city, which is a meeting place of Eastern and Western culture, lies the Sultan's Palace, Topkapi, with its great harem. And it is said of Inés' husband von Ribbing that he too keeps a harem. He married Inés when she was sixteen; he saved her father from bankruptcy, so to all intents and purposes he bought his wife. Inés feels such loathing for him that they have had no marital relations ever since he tried early in their marriage to compel her to do things she found disgusting. It is hinted that not only does he visit young girls, but also something even worse

– presumably a veiled reference to sexual activity with boys. Amalie Skram must have recalled the reaction to Constance's pronouncements comparing marriage to prostitution; she believed that her account of von Ribbing's harem-like arrangements would cause a similar revulsion. She wrote in a letter that she was afraid of being thrown into prison for having written the novel – a fate which had occurred to more than one of her contemporaries who had been found guilty of obscenity. But the fact that the events occurred in a foreign setting and that the novel was less clearly naturalistic meant that criticism was muted.

As a practising Roman Catholic, Inés cannot contemplate divorce. But her situation is so desperate, and she is so filled with longing for sexual fulfilment, that adultery is a natural and understandable choice. Even though she appears extremely coquettish and seductive, she has had only one lover in the course of her fourteen-year marriage. That affair was a disappointment. There is no moral censure from the narrator when Inés decides to embark on a relationship with the handsome, young and vulnerable Arthur Flemming. It is as if the narrator herself surrenders to the deep longing felt by the protagonist; surely at last she will succeed in experiencing what she thinks of as 'this mysterious rapture'. In this city, with its harem, its eunuchs, with riders on rearing horses in the streets and veiled women who have no rights at all, it seems right that Inés fights to experience union with another human being as salvation, as a renewal, as confirmation that she is after all alive and worthy of loving and being loved.

Yet the picture is a complex one. Who is Inés? She is not easy to understand, either for young Flemming or for the reader. She blows hot and cold, at one moment full of love and devotion, at the next unfeeling and dismissive. Borghild Krane, who was a psychiatrist as well as a literary reseacher, was the first to write an in-depth study of her; she characterizes Inés as calculating and egoistic, with an inner emptiness for which she compensates by striving for power over others. The character invites psychoanalytical interpretation. Inés is frigid, suggests Jorunn Hareide in her study; she does not want to give herself, to surrender her phallic position and lose control. Unni Langås writes that Inés exhibits features suggestive of a hysteric, who is split between male and female identity, and feels compelled to conceal the secrets of the body. She cannot reveal the truth, that she is unable to attain sexual fulfilment with her lover. According to Christine Hamm, Fru Inés should be seen as a transsexual, a woman who feels out of place in her own body. I myself have previously drawn attention to the fact that Inés experiences a fundamental lack, and that the descriptions of her are linked to images of castration: the eunuch, the mermaid in her dream and the flayed dog.

The complexity of the figure means that it is possible to interpret her in different ways. Skram places great emphasis on scenes of mirroring, and on the exchange of glances between Inés and Flemming. From a psychoanalytical viewpoint one might say that this reveals a narcissistic personality. Inés seeks confirmation of her own worth in Flemming's glance, and the two lovers feel that they can understand each other through an exchange of glances. In Flemming Inés is seeking not only the man who can love her; in his naiveté she sees also the innocent young girl she once was herself.

The novel is rich in images and symbols which constitute a solid basis for a psychoanalytical reading: a subterranean grotto, a funicular railway whose cable breaks when the lovers are sitting in it, graveyards, eunuchs, frisky horses and aggressive and tormented dogs. And portents and dreams. Yet psychoanalytical interpretations nevertheless leave something to be desired; do they really fully explain all the layers of Inés' personality? A reading of the novel which focuses on the city reveals that the author has not lost her touch for a realism which brings the setting to life, and that a consideration of this aspect contributes to a fuller understanding of the narrative. Constantinople is itself richly diverse; it consists of a Turkish section and a European section, and its population speaks a range of languages and belongs to different religions. The city's mosques have a complex history; Hagia Sofia was earlier the seat of the Eastern Orthodox church, then became a Roman Catholic cathedral, before it was transformed into a mosque during the Ottoman Empire in 1453. Like Inés herself, the city is full of contradictions and shifting moods and values. She too represents a mingling of east and west; she is introduced as a Levantine, in other words she comes from the Mediterranean coast of Asia. We are also told that her background is Spanish and Egyptian. With its mixture of white marble buildings and filthy backstreets, Constantinople is portrayed as both pure and impure, just like Inés. Her husband says he rescued her from a dungheap, but in the opening scene, sitting there in a white silk dress against the background of the town's white minarets, she represents purity. Life and death are never very far apart in this city, with its contrasts between the turbulent life of the streets and the quiet graveyards where lovers can meet.

The presence of eunuchs is a feature of the city; they can be seen everywhere. Early in the novel Inés tells the story of a woman who is punished because her husband has caught her being 'too familiar with a eunuch'. And Inés asks rhetorically: 'How could he be harmed by that?' Of the eunuch she states that he is whipped for an offence he has no concept of. De Amicis depicts eunuchs more sympathetically, and maintains that their dreadful fate leads to great suffering and deprivation. When Inés later in the novel wonders whether she is lacking in some way, it is suggested that she identifies with the castrated men whom she has every opportunity to observe at close quarters.

It is however in Inés' dream about a bleeding dog which lies at her feet that the connection between her and the city is most strongly expressed. She has dreamt about being loved by someone like the young Arthur Flemming, whom she at that point has only just met. Then her dream produces the image of 'a bloody, howling dog that dragged itself through filth and dry dust' before it lays its nose on Flemming's shoe. The dog changes into a mermaid, which is she herself, and thus she becomes the one who in the dream lays her face on his shoe before she dies. At the end of the novel she makes the trip to see a Greek abortionist, but changes her mind and walks away again. It is then she sees the flayed dog from her dreams being pursued through the streets by a pack of snarling dogs. An old man takes pity on it and places a saucepan lid over the bloody body, and the pack of dogs runs off. Here Inés' inner world becomes fused with the outer one; she recognises that she is the dog and like it she will die. She miscarries in a pool of blood, and a short time later dies at the country house.

More than anything else this scene demonstrates Skram's mastery. According to de Amicis' travelogue, the presence of dogs was oppressive in certain areas of Constantinople. He writes that they sleep in great heaps in the street. No-one owns them, and they function as a kind of refuse service; they are the street sweepers who eat all the rubbish and left-over food which is thrown into the streets. They guard their own area jealously, and never allow a strange dog to enter their territory; if one happens to do so, it is torn to pieces by the pack. They are the most persecuted of all creatures in the city, writes de Amicis, the wasted victims of hunger, war and love. They might move the very stones to pity.

Amalie Skram no doubt observed this, and she probably also read de Amicis' book. His account may have reawakened her own experiences and observations of the city. And she may have understood intuitively that the dogs could provide the perfect vehicle to embody Inés' character and also her fate, her experience of being an outcast.

There are in particular two aspects of the dogs, their uncleanness and their multiple function, that may have been of decisive importance. Inés' husband claims that he plucked her from 'a dungheap', a rubbish tip. And the fact that the dogs can arouse pity may have appealed to Skram. They are both victim and executioner, they are extremely aggressive but also subject to strict rules which govern their social behaviour, they live off rubbish but in that way keep the streets clean. To go to the dogs is an expression used by young Flemming. But the one who goes under may find mercy.

Does this depiction mean that Skram is venturing into symbolism? I do not believe that is a necessary interpretation. Just like Emile Zola, she understood that naturalism was not simply a photographic reproduction of reality. Realistic descriptions could be filled with myths and exaggerations, with images which broadened out the picture, which said something more universal about humanity's place in existence. For naturalists this was never an abstract concept, it was an insight which always needed to be anchored in a concrete event, a concrete place, at a precise time for a unique individual. In Constantinople, in the 1870s or 1880s, in a woman who has transgressed the boundaries drawn up for her life, a thirty-year-old woman who miscarries and will slowly bleed to death.

Liv Køltzow called *Fru Inés* a Passion story. A story of suffering and turbulent emotion, of risking everything and losing everything. But a Passion story also implies that the suffering has a meaning. And unlike Skram's other novels about love and marriage, I would suggest that here the suffering does lead to a possible redemption. The novel does not end in irreconcilable tragedy, as I myself suggested thirty years ago. The suffering Inés, like the flayed dog, finds mercy. Veiled women show her pity, offer her a drink, help her to her carriage. Whilst the husband at Lucie's deathbed in the novel of that name protests his innocence in her fate, here the husband asks the dying Inés for forgiveness for having married her. And Inés whispers 'Yes, yes', before her final words: 'Now the old man is bringing the *mangan* lid.'

The dogs – both as dream and as reality in the city of Constantinople – are the core of the story. They demonstrate that the outcast, suffering and dying themselves can feel pity, as when Inés for the first time can think of her husband with mildness and sympathy. And when the dog's story is placed alongside that of Inés, it shows even more emphatically that the outcast and the dying will also find mercy. Behind all this suffering and striving there is in fact forgiveness, mercy and redemption.

Irene Engelstad

# Bibliography

## Istanbul

Ayse Yetiskin Kubilay: *Maps of Istanbul, 1422-1922*. Istanbul 2009.

Auldjo, John: *Journal of a Visit to Constantinople and Some of the Greek Islands in the Summer of 1833*. Kindle edition, 2012.

Celic, Zeynep: *The Remaking of Istanbul: Portrait of an Ottoman City in the Nineteenth Century*. Seattle 1986.

Crawford, Frances Marion: *Constantinople*. 1893, Kindle edition, 2012.

De Amicis, Edmondo: *Constantinople*. New York 1878. Published in Danish as *Konstantinopel*. Copenhagen 1888.

Mansel, Philip: *Constantinople. City of the World's Desire, 1453-1924*. London 1995.

Mansel, Philip: *Levant. Splendour and Catastrophe on the Mediterranean*. New Haven & London 2010.

Montagu, Lady Mary Wortley: *The Turkish Embassy Letters*. London 1995.

Stoddard, John L: *Lectures*, v. 2: *Constantinople, Jerusalem, Egypt*. New York 1897, revised edition 1911.

Von Tietz, Fredrich: *St. Petersburgh, Constantinople, and Napoli di Romania in 1833 and 1834, vol II*. London 1833.

## Amalie Skram

Engelstad, Irene, 1984: *Sammenbrudd og gjennombrudd. Amalie Skrams romaner om ekteskap og sinnssykdom.* Oslo 1984.

Engelstad, Irene and Ingrid Wad: 'Kjærlighetens, lystens og dødens offer. En lesning av Amalie Skrams *Fru Inés.*' *Amalie Skram Årbok.* Amalie Skram selskapet, Bergen 2013.

Garton, Janet: *Norwegian Women's Writing 1850-1990.* London 1993.

Garton, Janet: 'Efterskrift', Det Danske Sprog og Litteraturselskab's edition of *Constance Ring*, Borgen, Copenhagen 2007.

Garton, Janet: *Amalie. Et forfatterliv.* Oslo 2011.

Hamm, Christine: *Medlidenhet og melodrama: Amalie Skrams romaner om ekteskap.* Bergen 2006.

Hareide, Jorunn: 'Kokettens hemmelighet: En psykoanalytisk lesning av Amalie Skrams *Fru Inés.*' *Edda* 2 1987: 109-120.

Krane, Borghild: *Amalie Skram og kvinnens problem.* Oslo 1951.

Køltzow, Liv: *Den unge Amalie Skram. Et portrett fra det nittende århundre.* Oslo 1992.

Langås, Unni: 'Marmorkvinnen. Den forstenede kroppen i Skrams *Fru Inés.*' In *Kroppens betydning i norsk litteratur. 1800-1900*, pp. 188-214. Bergen 2004.

Wad, Ingrid: *En Constance i Konstantinopel.* Institutt for lingvistiske og nordiske studier, University of Oslo 2007.

# Image Credits

p. 7      *Plan of Constantinople* by  C. Stolpe,1882
          Bibliothèque nationale de France

p. 11     *Monastery, Princes' Islands,* Steel engraving
          *Constantinople and its Environs:* Fisher & Son, 1838.

p. 55     *Constantinople,* Postcard, undated  (ca. 1905)

p. 59     *Constantinople - Quay of Galata,* Postcard,
          undated (ca.1914 )

p. 63     *The Eastern Question: The Grande Rue De Pera*
          *The Graphic,* May 13, 1876

p. 75     *Pera, Constantinople,* Postcard, undated

p. 83     *Therapia, Bosphorus,* from *Lectures, v.2*
          John L. Stoddard, 1905

p. 87     *Turkish woman in cemetery at Skutari opposite*
          *Constantinople,* Photograph, 1909 -1919
          Library of Congress Prints and Photographs Division
          Washington, D.C. 20540 USA

p. 109    *Kara-Keui (Galata) bridge, Constantinople*
          Postcard 1890-1900
          United States Library of Congress

AMALIE SKRAM

# *Lucie*

## (translated by Katherine Hanson & Judith Messick)

This novel from 1888 tells the story of the misalliance between Lucie, a vivacious dancing girl from Tivoli, and Theodor Gerner, a respectable lawyer from the strait-laced middle-class society of nineteenth-century Norway.

Having first kept her as a mistress, Gerner is so captivated by Lucie that he marries her, only to discover that his project to turn her into a demure housewife is continually frustrated by her irrepressible sensuality and lack of breeding. What had made her alluring as a mistress makes her unacceptable as a wife.

ISBN 9781870041485
UK £8.95
(Paperback, 168 pages)

HELENE URI

## *Honey Tongues*

(translated by Kari Dickson)

The honey tongues of the title belong to four friends in their thirties who have known each other since school. They make up a 'sewing circle' where no sewing is done, but much exquisite food is lovingly prepared and consumed and increasingly bitchy gossip exchanged.

The novel follows their three-weekly meetings over six months, as they take turns to entertain each other; we are privy to their thoughts and memories and discover how apparently innocent actions are motivated by emotional hang-ups with their roots in childhood traumas. The tension builds towards a gourmet trip to Copenhagen to celebrate their friendship, where during an eight-course meal the masks drop and undisguised fear and loathing are revealed. Shocking secrets are unearthed as the balance of power subtly shifts from one member of the group to another. Brilliantly observed, this is female bonding at its worst, manipulative and psychotic, exposing the dependency and deceit behind the compassionate and affectionate façade.

ISBN 9781870041720
UK £9.95
(Paperback, 192 pages)

SVAVA JAKOBSDÓTTIR

# Gunnlöth's Tale

(translated by Oliver Watts)

This spirited and at times sinister novel ensnares the reader in a tangled encounter between modern-day Scandinavia and the ancient world of myth. In the 1980s, a hardworking Icelandic businesswoman and her teenage daughter Dís, who has been arrested for apparently committing a strange and senseless robbery, are unwittingly drawn into a ritual-bound world of goddesses, sacrificial priests, golden thrones, clashing crags and kings-in-waiting. It is said that Gunnlöth was seduced by Odin so he could win the 'mead' of poetry from her, but is that really true, and why was Dís summoned to their world?

The boundaries dissolve and the parallels between Gunnlöth's circle and the strange company into which Dís's mother is drawn as she fights to clear Dís's name grow ever closer. The earth-cherishing goddess seems set on a collision course with strategic thinker Odin who has discovered that iron can be extracted from the marshes where she resides, and environmental disaster also looms in the modern context, brought into sharp focus by a shocking world event.

ISBN 9781870041799
UK £9.95
(Paperback, 232 pages)

JØRGEN-FRANZ JACOBSEN

# *Barbara*

(translated by George Johnston)

Originally written in Danish, *Barbara* was the only novel by the
Faroese author Jørgen-Frantz Jacobsen (1900-38), yet it quickly
achieved international best-seller status and is still one of the best-
loved classics of Danish and Faroese literature. On the face of it,
Barbara is a straightforward historical romance. It contains a story
of passion in an exotic setting with overtones of semi-piracy; there
is a powerful erotic element, an outsider who breaks up a marriage,
and a built-in inevitability resulting from Barbara's own psychological
make-up. She stands as one of the most complex female characters
in modern Scandinavian literature: beautiful, passionate, devoted,
amoral and uncomprehending of her own tragedy. Jørgen-Frantz
Jacobsen portrays her with fascinated devotion.

ISBN 9781870041225
UK £9.95
(Paperback, 304 pages)

Lightning Source UK Ltd.
Milton Keynes UK
UKOW04f0600130314

228050UK00001B/2/P

9 781909 408050